CHAPTER 1

This is how I got mixed up with Albertina Legge.

The funeral had just ended and Dad was standing outside St. Cuthbert's Church doing his bereaved-but-stoic-son routine. (A firm handshake, a smiley frown, but no tears. Tears are extra.)

I was beside him doing my bereaved-but-stoic-grandson thing, which consisted of me staring sadly at my shoes and fantasizing about Kirsten Falkenham in that T-shirt with the see-through back.

I think it was Perry Roy's funeral but—weird, considering how this would totally change my life—I'm not sure. Could have been Bob Doggett's. In my defense, we do a lot of funerals and these old guys are hard enough to tell apart at the best of times, let alone when they're in a box.

We heard, "Excuse me, excuse me, if you don't mind, excuse me," and an old lady in a wheelchair made her way through the smokers towards us.

She put her hand on her heart. "Lovely eulogy," she said to Dad. "You truly captured the essence of the man."

Dad smiled. A real smile. He takes pride in his work. The lady smiled back.

That was Albertina. She'd be dead soon, but you'd never have known it. If anything, she seemed a tad *too* alive—fuchsia lips, hair like Marge Simpson's only in a tasteful shade of tangerine, not to mention a good fifteen inches of wrinkly cleavage that made me think of the mighty Amazon snaking its way down the relief map I made in Mr. Jackman's geography class.

Dad said, "He was a special man. One of a kind."

"One of a kind?" Albertina raised her orange eyebrows. "Strange. I could have sworn you gave the exact same eulogy last week, just before you sent Don Friesen to the boneyard."

For a second, Dad looked like he'd been tasered, but he pulled himself together pretty fast.

"They were both good men," he managed to squeak out through his nostrils.

"Yeah. Cloning is getting better all the time." Albertina had a cackle over that. The smokers turned to see what was so funny.

Dad pretended he was in on the joke too—just a couple friends sharing another wonderful memory of the dead guy—and whispered, "May I ask who you are?"

"Sure. Just let me get my badge out here . . ." She started rooting through her purse.

"Beg your pardon? You want to get out of here?" Dad was smiling like a politician who'd just been caught with a crack pipe. "Let me help you." He grabbed the handles of her wheelchair and pushed her down the disabled ramp at a speed just short of qualifying time for the NASCAR circuit. I did my best to keep up.

"There are two things you should know about me before you plan your next move," she said as we crossed the parking lot. "One: I'm a trained hog-caller. Perhaps you've heard of me. Albertina Legge—two e's, two g's. Got a wall full of trophies. Your son here—if he is your son and I'm sure as hell not convinced of that yet—might like to see them some day. Until then, I'm just warning you, I have a very loud voice if I need to use it."

"You won't," Dad mewled. (Sadly, that was the only word for it.) "You won't."

"No. I don't think I will, especially once you know the second thing about me." She batted her false eyelashes, then dropped her voice an octave or two. "I'm armed."

She reached into her cleavage like she was pulling out a gun. That's when I got scared. Who knew what she was packing in there?

Dad did one of those ho-ho-ho-middle-aged-dad

laughs, but I could tell he was scared too. "No need for that. Why don't we just get you into the shade where it's not so hot?"

"I don't find it hot, myself." Albertina patted the frills on her blouse back into place. "But my guess is you do. You're sweating like a high-wire walker in a typhoon."

Dad wheeled her under a big tree at the edge of the parking lot. He wanted her out of earshot of the eight other people who'd managed to pry themselves off their leatherette recliners to go to Perry's funeral. (Or was it Bob's?)

She stretched her legs out on her footrest. She was wearing bright-pink stilettos, which struck me as an odd choice of shoes for someone in a wheelchair, or at a funeral for that matter.

"Okay. Enough of the charade, boys. What's your racket?"

"It's not a racket. Honest." Dad and I both nodded like we were riding over a bumpy road in a go-cart.

"Please. Don't let my pert little figure fool you. I wasn't born yesterday. I know a scam when I see one. You cozying up to lonely old geezers just before they kick the bucket, then hightailing it with their money? That the deal? Maybe even helping them on their way a bit?"

"No." Dad somehow found his grown-up voice again.

"No. It's nothing like that. That's not why we're here. I'll show you." He reached into the breast pocket of his suit.

"Hands in the air, fella!" Albertina clearly wasn't fooling about those hog-calling trophies. Dad threw his hands up. A guy helping his wife into a big boat of a Chevrolet waved back.

"I warned you, buster. I'm armed."

"I was just getting my wallet." Dad was mewling again. "That's all. I just wanted to show you my business card."

She looked at Dad. She thought about it for a second. "Okay. But I've got my sights trained on your son, here—if he is your son. Try anything funny and he's the first to go."

Dad really was sweating now, which surprised me. He gets his armpits Botoxed so that usually isn't a problem.

He eased out his wallet as if it were a bomb that could explode at any second and held it open for her. "See? That's us."

I don't know why he insisted on carrying around that cheesy Sears family portrait. It was taken sometime in the middle of the Paleogoofball era when it was still okay to appear in public sporting a kiddy-mohawk, a fluorescent-yellow beater, and technicolour delusions about just how cool you are.

"Cute," Albertina said. "So you're related. Doesn't mean you're not criminals."

"We aren't." Dad handed her his card. "We're a legitimate business. Our Chamber of Commerce certification number is at the bottom."

Her glasses were hanging around her neck. She put them on the end of her nose and her eyeballs ballooned to fill the lenses.

"Almost Family Surrogate Agency," she read. "What the hell is this?"

Dad got his groove back. "We provide substitute relatives for all manner of engagements: weddings, funerals, corporate functions, or simple companionship. Our employees' discretion and warm personal demeanour make them—"

"What? Tell me you're kidding." Albertina's glasses landed on her chest with a *splop*. "Rent-a-relative?"

"Well, we prefer to—"

"Is that what this is? Some pathetic schmuck pays you to be pretend to be family?"

"None of our clients are in any way—"

"I'm right. Oh, lord leaping. Now I've heard everything. And here I took you for scam artists." She barked, or maybe that was just the way she laughed. "This ain't a scam, it's just some hare-brained scheme."

Dad straightened his tie. "I'll have you know we provide a valuable service—"

"Fake families? Right. So who's the genius running

this business empire?" Albertina held up her glasses and squinted at the name on the card. "William Redden? That you?"

Dad nodded and looked away, chin in the air. She'd insulted him and his company.

"Good golly." Albertina banged the arm of her wheelchair. "Not *the* William Redden? Will Redden? From *Up to No Good*?"

Dad and I both rotated towards her in slo-mo. I know his heart was pounding as hard as mine was. I could hear it.

"It is!" She gave another big laugh. Dad's face went a colour normally only seen on hairless mole rats. "I *knew* I'd seen you before."

Weird that after all these years, it would be Albertina Legge who recognized him.

CHAPTER 2

For anyone born in this century, some explanation may be required.

Up to No Good was a sitcom, wildly, if briefly, popular fifteen years ago. You know the type. Four lovable misfits start a window-cleaning business solely to get a better look at the hot blonde working on the top floor of the MegaBank office tower. Hijinks ensue.

Lame, I know, but no one cared. The producers figured people would watch anything starring the guys from Nu Luv. (Some explanation is no doubt required here too. Boy band. One pouty. One smiley. One squinty. Their big, by which I mean *only*, hit: "U R . . . My Heart.")

The producers were right. People did watch—but instead of falling for Kody, Kelton, or Diego, everyone went nuts for the obese, bucktoothed sidekick they'd lovingly nicknamed "The Bloater." You can still find fanny packs at yard sales printed with his hilarious catchphrase, "That's maniacal!"

Up to No Good ran for a couple of seasons before Nu Luv split up. (They got in a big fight about money or hairstyles or something.) Bloat wasn't sorry to see it go. There are only so many fat jokes one man can stand, plus the producers were already planning a spinoff series for him. He went out and got his stomach stapled, his teeth straightened, and the lump on his nose Brad-Pitted right out of existence.

The show, *Who You Calling Bloat?*, was supposed to be a big hit, but someone's aim was a little off. Turned out audiences liked Bloat better fat. Sure, he was good-looking now, but good-looking the way guys who model stain-resistant workwear in the weekly Walmart flyer are good-looking. Totally forgettable.

Bloat's show tanked. His marriage to one of his co-stars tanked. He got a few commercials for a high-fibre burrito and a man-girdle, but after a while, they tanked too.

His wife ditched him and their kid, and got big in Australia. (No, she wasn't the hot blonde. She was the scrawny short-order cook the Nu Luv boys kept trying to set Bloat up with. Opposites attract and all that.) Bloat hit the road. He stopped driving just before he ran out of money, found a cheap place to live, and turned into the guy I fondly refer to as Dad.

It's not much of a family, if you can even call it a

family. There's just the two of us, plus Mum, who almost never forgets to send me birthday cards from Down Under—but that's life. Things were tough for a while. Royalties from the show had dried up, and we were living on the only acting job Dad could get—as a pirate with a parrot Velcroed to his shoulder, taking sloppy drunks on Ye Olde Brewery tours. I think he found it pretty depressing. (I kept discovering piles of Nutty Buddy wrappers in the saddest places. Behind the toilet. In the Weetabix box. Stuffed in a flashlight where the batteries are supposed to go.)

Then, five years ago, right before our Internet was going to get cut off, he got an email from Ms. Aiko Nara from The Asia-Pacific *Up to No Good* Fan Club in Sapporo, Japan. She realized he was "very much in demand" and apologized for contacting him directly. Her many attempts to reach his agent had gone unanswered (no doubt because his agent didn't remember who he was). Ms. Nara went on to say how deeply honoured her fan club would be to host Mr. Bloat on a two-week promotional tour of Japan whenever his schedule allowed.

Dad didn't want to seem too desperate, so he counted backwards from one hundred before responding. Whaddya know? He just happened to be available immediately. Ms. Nara was delighted.

He parked me at a neighbour's and took off. I don't remember ever seeing him so happy. *Up to No Good* had been huge in Japan. He just needed to get a few things straightened out, then he'd bring me to live in Sapporo too. This was going to be the start of The Bloater's big comeback.

Spoiler alert: it wasn't. Fans over there didn't like skinny Bloat any better than fans over here did, and Dad couldn't eat enough tempura in two weeks to make them change their minds.

The good news is Aiko Nara turned out to be pretty nice. After she finally figured out who Dad was—she kept asking him when Mr. Bloat was arriving—they became good friends. He told her all his problems. She's the one who suggested he start a relative-rental business. They're common in Japan, she said, and he was just unmemorable enough now to pull one off here.

So, long story short, we didn't get to move to Japan, but we did get to keep our Internet connection. Dad's been running Almost Family ever since.

We make an okay living. Dad has regular acting work again—that's how he spins it for his parents on the off chance they phone from whatever elder cruise they're on at the moment—and I've got a part-time job that doesn't require wearing a hairnet or a hot-dog costume. Pews are hard on my bony butt, but on the plus side, anything that happens in a church—weddings, funerals, exorcisms, for all I know—includes sandwiches with the crusts cut off. I'd say Almost Family lets us meet lots of great people too, but then I'd be lying. Frankly, there's usually a reason their relatives don't friend these guys on Facebook.

All in all, though, not a bad gig. The only thing we have to be careful about is making sure no one recognizes us as rentals. That would kill our business.

Which is why we gulped when Albertina Legge dropped the *Up to No Good* line in St. Cuthbert's parking lot. We thought we were done for.

"So how much you charge for your so-called services?" she said, after milking our agony for a while.

I could see Dad bristle at that, but he ain't proud. The power bill was due in three days.

"Thirty-five dollars an hour for me, fifty for the two of us. We also have a roster of other associates, including those suitable for aunts, uncles, daughters, cousins—"

"How much just for the kid?"

"Cam?"

"That's his name? What's it short for? Chameleon?" She thought she was pretty clever.

"Cameron. He doesn't do solo jobs."

She shrugged like some old-time mobster. "What do you think I'm going to do to him? He's a foot taller than me, and like I said, don't let my snazzy little figure fool you. I'm an elderly lady."

"Sorry. He's not for rent."

"Is he for sale then?"

Dad glared at her.

"I'm joking. You were funnier when you were fat." Albertina clearly knew how to pick people's scabs. "Fine. You don't want my business, then so long, boys. It's been swell. Haven't laughed this hard since the *Up to No Good* finale."

Albertina flicked the business card over her shoulder then wheeled her way back across the parking lot to a lime-green subcompact. I figured that was the last we'd see of her, and frankly, that was A-OK by me.

CHAPTER 3

This is how I got mixed up with Raylene Let's-Say-Butler.

It was a Monday, which is usually our pulled-pork poutine night, but Dad had a high-school reunion to go to. (Not his own, of course. Some lady's. She wanted to show up with a hotter husband than the one she was actually married to. Apparently, there was a former cheerleader who needed to be put in her place.)

My buddy Suraj had gotten off early from his job at the deli and dropped by with dinner. He's allowed to take anything home that's stale, mouldy, or has been sneezed on more than the regulation six times. Our buffet that evening consisted of some crushed spanakopita, week-old dim sum, questionable pad Thai, and the puckered end of a mortadella sausage. My mouth was delirious.

Dad appeared in the doorway to his bedroom wearing a grey fitted jacket, jeans, and a stick-on 'stache.

"So?" he said.

Before I had a chance to collect my thoughts, Suraj said, "Porn-star-wannabe."

Dad nodded and went back to try again.

Everyone has a special talent, and that's Suraj's. He can take one look and sum up the impression a person makes in a pithy three-to-five words. It sometimes hurts, but it's always valuable.

After several variations on hair and wardrobe— "Too-scientolgist," "Bodies-in-the-basement," and my favourite, "Red-elf-on-the-Rice-Krispies-box" Dad settled on a brown leather jacket, horn-rimmed glasses, and the porn-star jeans for the hint of sexy his client seemed to be after.

Suraj's response: "J. Crewed it right out of the park, Wolfman." (Suraj is the only person to call Dad Wolfman. It's a long story—glue-on chest hair, barbecue lighter, trip to the emergency room—not worth going into here.)

Dad grabbed his cheat sheet of important names and aimed a finger-gun at me. "Bed before dawn."

"Whatever."

"Look after him for me, would ya, Surge?"

Suraj rubbed his hands together and snickered. "Yes, master. As you wish."

With Dad out of the way, Suraj and I played chess and talked about Albertina. She'd left a threatening message on our voice mail that afternoon, something about Almost Family not conforming to government health regulations. I hadn't mentioned it to Dad. He was rattled enough by her as it was, and I didn't want him blowing the reunion gig. We needed the income.

"I thought you said Albertina was, like, ninety or something?" Suraj took my rook with his pawn. "So, you're breaking a couple of health rules. What's she going to do about it? Not like she's a cop."

"I don't know. She said she had a badge."

"You see it?"

"Right. Like we want her pulling a badge out in front of the minister. Reverend Muncaster gives us half our referrals," I said, then I screamed in agony.

Suraj had just catapulted my rook into the overhead light fixture. (We'd updated some of the traditional rules of chess to make the game more interesting. Normally, the field goal was one of my favourite modifications.)

"What are you going to do about it?" I presumed he was talking about Albertina's threat and not my rook. It would rattle around in there with the others until someone got the ladder out or it melted, which was more likely.

"She said to be at the Spring Garden Professional Centre at ten tomorrow morning, or prepare to be sorry."

"That's what she said—'or prepare to be sorry'?"

I shrugged. "Her dialogue's even worse than yours." Suraj had an eight-part sci-fi series he'd been writing since elementary school.

He didn't like that. He took my queen off the board and biffed her into the light fixture too, so I winged a handful of pad Thai at his head and he lunged over the table and roundhoused me in the ear. Next thing you know, we were whaling away at each other the same way we do every time we get together.

He's puny but determined, and I was face down in a pool of plum sauce when the doorbell rang. I leapt at the chance to call the fight.

"Get off me, would you? Pick this stuff up. I'll deal with her." Lynette Mc-Something-or-Other lives in the basement apartment and is always padding upstairs in her hand-knit slippers and polar fleece sweats to complain about "excessive noise," by which she means anything louder than a suppressed burp.

I wiped the sauce off my forehead and headed to the door. I had this down to a science. I'd apologize and promise not to do it again, then make some lame joke about boys being boys, at which point Lynette would apologize for her hypersensitive hearing (which always sounded like bragging to me) and I'd stand there nodding until she gave up trying to see if Dad was home and padded back downstairs.

I put a "my-bad" smile on my face and opened the door.

Lynette is about five-foot-nothing, so I had my head pre-bent to talk to her. This would explain how I found myself eyeball-to-eyeball with a small-to-medium pair of breasts in a camo tank top.

The owner cleared her throat and they jiggled. I looked up with a start. A girl about sixteen—short silver hair, black-framed glasses, and a nose ring—said, "Almost Family?"

I stared back blankly. On the upside, at least it was at her face this time.

"Is this the office of Almost Family?"

Still not computing.

She stepped back to look at the street number, then checked the scrunched-up business card in her hand. "5508 Robie Street, Suite 1A. Maybe that's supposed to be 5503." She smudged some mud off the card and shook her head.

"No, that's the right address." Suraj had materialized beside me. He managed to sound remarkably professional, despite the noodles festooning his head. "May I help you?"

She put a hand on her hip and curled her lip. I thought she was going to up and leave, but she just gave us the once-over, then went, "Yeah. I'd like to rent a brother."

She took a noodle off Suraj's ear and stepped past us into the international headquarters of Almost Family. Suraj and I bugged our eyes out at each other and mouthed several versions of *Whadda we do now?* To the best of my knowledge, Lynette Whatchamacallit was the only female ever to have acknowledged our presence.

Suraj gave a panicky shrug, then followed the breast-owner inside. I checked my pits, then went in too. She was standing in the middle of the room, looking around as if she was trying to choose a new paint colour or figure out where the smell was coming from, either of which would have been appreciated. Suraj beetled in front of her and swept some meal-sized crumbs off the futon and onto the floor.

"Sit. Please sit. Excuse the mess. We were developing some team-building exercises for one of our clients."

Suraj isn't on the payroll so I'm not exactly sure why he was taking over the interview, other than, of course, he's Suraj and his lips were still working.

She found a dry, relatively stain-free spot and sat.

I perched on one arm of the only chair we have. Suraj perched on the other. We must have looked like hosts for a preschool program about to launch into some ditty about the difference between left and right. I was sorry there wasn't a manlier option but my leg was jiggling too much to stand.

Suraj said, "May I ask how you heard about Almost Family?"

"I didn't." Her voice was sort of husky.

Sort of Scarlett-Johansson-with-a-chest-cold.

Sort of Oh-my-God-I-can't-believe-she's-actually-talking-to-us.

"Then how is it you found us?" Suraj picked a pad of paper off the coffee table to record the information. It would have looked like a totally businesslike thing to do if the paper hadn't been a Scattergories scoresheet.

"Found your card on the street. Thought it was garbage." She sounded like she still did. "Why do you need to know?"

"No reason. Just, like, market research, whatever. Perhaps we could start by getting your name?"

"Raylene."

"And how do you spell that?"

She sighed like *what's with all the questions?* "Whatever's easy."

I could see that appealed to Suraj. He'd no doubt be using it himself when school started up again in the fall. You can just imagine what some poor substitute teacher would come up with for Suraj Bandodpadhyay.

"And your last name?"

She sighed again, checked out the movie poster we had covering the hole Suraj's head had made in the wall a few weeks back, then scratched the side of her nose.

"Let's say Butler."

"Let's-Say-Butler. Is that a hyphenated name?" He was making a joke but Raylene either missed it or chose to ignore it.

"So how do I pick a brother? Got a website or something?"

"No. No website. As you can imagine, anonymity is very important in our business," Suraj said. "You tell us what you need and we'll match your requirements."

He didn't say, "... as long as you're looking for someone just like Cam." Dad had a few old acting buddies on the roster and even a couple former clients, but I was the only preteen/teen/juvenile/young adult male we had on offer at the moment. That's why I was somewhat surprised when Suraj went on to say, "Can you tell us what you're looking for exactly? Height? Hair colour? Cafeteria clique: nerd, jock, hipster, foreign exchange student?"

"I'm not picky." Our kind of client.

"Age? We offer everything from a slightly balding older brother to a mechanical windup baby you can carry around in a custom-designed Snugli." He totally made that last one up on the spot.

"Fifteen and a half. Or sixteen, if he can pass." Bingo. Direct hit.

Suraj scribbled something official-looking onto the scoresheet.

"And what will you require him for? A business event? Family gathering? TV engagement? Oddly enough, we're . . ."

Raylene stood up. "On second thought, forget it. I wasn't expecting the third degree." She was at the door in a flash.

"Sorry!" Suraj raced after her. "I was merely attempting to ensure we satisfied your needs. If more discretion is preferred, we'll gladly . . ."

The door could be hard to open if you didn't know the trick. Raylene was yanking away at it as if she were the next victim in *Saw V*.

The latch gave way. She staggered back. She was going to leave forever.

"I can be your brother," I said.

She turned and looked at me. Her eyes were brown but there was a green stripe in the right one. "You talk?" she said.

"Sometimes. When I get a chance."

She almost smiled, although I could tell she didn't mean to.

Suraj said, "Or if you'd prefer something slightly more exotic, I'm also available."

Raylene didn't respond. For a while there, she

looked like she had a sore tooth, but maybe she was just considering the options. She finally said, "I actually need a twin, so I should probably go with the white kid. Too much explaining to do otherwise. What'll it cost?"

"Thirty-five dollars an hour." What was Suraj thinking? What fifteen-and-a-half-year-old has that kind of money to waste on a brother?

"Except this week," I said, "when new clients get the first ten hours absolutely free."

I sounded a bit more like the guy on the ShamWow! infomercial than I'd meant to. She almost smiled again, and if I wasn't in love before, I was now.

"I'll only take five free hours," she said. "After that, if I like you, I'll pay. I'm good for it."

I nodded. She wrote my cell phone number on her hand and said she'd be in touch. I controlled myself until I saw her disappear around the corner of Robie and Bliss, then I jumped and squealed as if I'd just been crowned Miss World.

CHAPTER 4

Suraj was doing his thing again. "Claims-to-be-fifty-percent-anime-on-her-mother's-side."

I stuck my foot in his face.

"That's Raylene Let's-Say-Butler to a T and you know it," he said around my sock. "You're just mad because I nailed it."

He tried again. "Secretly-addicted-to-*Say-Yes-to-the-Dress*."

"Why are you even bothering, Suraj?"

"Devoted-last-eighteen-months-to-writing-spiteful-three-chord-songs-about-her-ex-boyfriend."

"If you dislike her so much, what was that offer of 'something slightly more exotic' all about?"

"Just looking out for you, bro."

I pushed him off the futon. He landed on the floor with a *crunch* but kept talking. "You obviously liked her—which was painful enough to witness—but to like someone who would actually *pay* you to be her brother is a crime against decency. Major ick-factor, if you ask me."

"Which luckily I didn't. You're just pissed she chose me."

"Like the girl said, she's not picky." He lay on his back and put his decomposing feet on the coffee table. "So what are you going to do with her when she calls?"

"No clue. What do I know about brothers? I mean, other than what I see on TV, and brothers there are always either evil, stupid, or just, like, I don't know, walking garburators or something."

"Why, darling, you're a shoo-in for the role!"

I flicked the remains of a pork bun at him. "You got a sister. Any suggestions?"

"I'd say cut her food up for her and let her play with wrapping paper. But Charu is two. That might not work with Has-a-pet-ferret."

I had a feeling he was right but I had no idea what *would* work. Raylene was a mystery to me. Even more than most girls, and that's saying something.

The whole "Let's say Butler" business? What's with that? Showing up at the apartment? Clients never just show up at the apartment. Acting all dodgy anytime Suraj asked her anything? How much could a fifteen-year-old possibly have to hide?

Those questions were nothing, of course, compared to the big one.

"Why would someone rent a brother?" I said. "I get the old folks wanting relatives to visit them in the seniors' home. I even get why that lady would want someone like Dad to bring to her high school reunion. But what does some teenage girl need a brother for? Most girls I know are looking to get rid of their brothers."

"You know some girls? When did that happen?"

"Okay, no. But I have heard them talk in the hallway, and my question remains: Why would Raylene want a brother?"

"To beat up some guy who's giving her a hard time?"

"Oh. Right. And I'm just the raging he-man for that. I can't even beat *you* up. She'd be better off sicking Charu on him."

Suraj made some joke about the kid's lethal drool output, then his eyes went big. "I know. Organ donation. Raylene wants your organs, bro. That's what this is all about."

He wasn't kidding—and he was quite excited about the possibility too. (No doubt, it would show up as a storyline in his Plasmic Defenders series soon.) I let him yammer on about blood matches and tissue rejection and what you can get for a nice juicy kidney these days. Truth is, I didn't really care why Raylene Let's-Say-Butler wanted me. She had me.

CHAPTER 5

I was going to tell Dad about Raylene when he got back from the reunion but I—

No. Sorry. That's a lie. I had no intention of *ever* telling Dad about Raylene. By agreeing to be her brother, I was breaking two of the most important rules of Almost Family.

No freebies except for Actual Family, which, given our circumstances, means no freebies at all. It's just too easy to feel sorry for people. And—

No solo gigs for anyone under twenty-one. In other words, me. Dad's terrified of "some perv trying something," and frankly there's nothing creepier than a middle-aged man saying "perv," so normally I'd be terrified of a solo gig too. When a single guy needs a nephew to show a lady friend his fatherly ways, Dad always arranges to be bowling in the next alley or golfing at the next tee or staking out the joint somehow—a consequence of which is that most people assume *he's* the perv.

It didn't seem very likely that Raylene would be trying something on me, but like the old folks say, hope springs eternal. I wasn't going to blow my chances by telling Dad.

He strolled in just after midnight and picked up the other controller. "How was your night?" he said before killing my shogun. (There's a lot of downtime when you're shooting a TV show, so his years on *Up to No Good* weren't a total waste. Dad's a much more lethal player than your average forty-three-year-old.)

I shrugged, then jerked my head towards the lump on the floor formerly known as Suraj.

"Do his parents know he's here?"

"Where else would he be? And yes." The Bandodpadhyays have four other boys plus Charu, all stuffed into an apartment half the size of ours. You'd think they'd be thrilled to have one less body for a while, but they watch Suraj like a hawk. No doubt Mr. B would be round by six the next morning to take a urine sample.

Dad sneezed and I managed to execute one of his samurais while he was getting back on his feet. I asked about his night.

"Ain't *Hamlet* but it pays the bills," he said.

"You've used that line before."

"And I'll use it again."

"Nice lady?"

"To me? Yeah. They're all nice to me. Still, gotta wonder what kind of person wants to fork over two hundred and ten bucks plus tax just to stick it to some girl who offended her twenty-five years ago. So much for forgive and forget."

That makes Dad sound like a really decent person, but you have to put it into perspective. He was systematically massacring my entire army while he said it.

"Yeah, well. Whaddya expect?" I said.

He threw down his controller and slumped on the futon. "Wasn't a surprise, but jeez. I'd take lonely and depressed over spiteful and mean any day. I kind of like the lonely gigs. Makes me feel like I'm helping make the world a better place . . ."

"Yeah. You're a regular little Mother Teresa, you are."

"Okay. Laugh—but it's true, sorta. Bob Doggett's son hadn't found the time to see him in years. I played cribbage with the old guy twice a week for a few months and he died a happy man. No shame in that. But tonight, slow dancing over and over again past some sorry ex-cheerleader? That just made me feel like a jerk. I hate doing people's dirty work."

"So don't do it anymore."

He looked at me over his fake glasses. "You want to go back to no-name Froot Loops?"

"Nooooo! Not the dreaded Frooty Zeros!"

"Yes, my friend. Zero taste! Zero crunch! Zero reason to enjoy! Sound good? Didn't think so. Which is why I still do spiteful. Not to mention miserable, delusional, bitter or—my favourite—the combo pack."

"Could be worse."

This was one of our games.

"Could be. I could be in leopard-print spandex and a glue-on tail, playing one of the backup kittens in *Cats*."

"Could be Pirate Ned again with a boot full of someone else's vomit."

"Could be the guy in the hot tub on that diarrhea commercial."

"Could be Suraj with red lips and bright blue eye shadow." I let that sink for a moment.

"Could be indeed," Dad said and waggled an eyebrow at me.

He took Suraj's shoulders, I took his feet, and we put him on the futon. The great thing about our business is that we have the resources to make anything we imagine possible. We raided the makeup kit and gave Suraj the full flamenco dancer—eyes, lips, big white flower behind his ear, even a couple of well-developed tennis balls down his shirt. The guy didn't budge. (I'm never sure until morning if he's asleep or if rigor mortis has set in.)

We took a couple of pictures and sent them to his father. Mr. B's got our whole series tacked behind the cash register at his vacuum repair shop—Suraj with the baby bonnet and soother, Suraj with the ratty beard and scar, Suraj with the antlers and flashing red nose. That stuff totally cracks him up.

When we'd finished the photo shoot, Dad tucked a blanket over Suraj and we went to bed.

I don't know if it was because I was worried about getting in trouble or because I was worried about returning to a life of no-name cereal, but I didn't mention Albertina to Dad then either.

CHAPTER 6

The next day, I got to the coffee shop in the lobby of the Spring Garden Professional Centre just before ten. Albertina was sitting at a table near the back, waving a claw at me.

"You alone?" She craned her neck as if she were casing the place for undercover agents. (Like *way* undercover. The place was totally empty.) "Good. I was hoping it'd just be you. Not sure The Bloater has the constitution for this type of thing."

She held up her half-empty glass and hollered, "Waiter!"

The teenaged guy behind the sandwich counter looked up from his cell phone and sighed.

"Another one of these for me, please and thank you," she said, "and bring us something pink and fizzy for my grandson here."

"Uh . . . this is self-serve? I think we've discussed that before?"

"Much obliged!" She turned back to me and smiled the way teachers do just before they give you the I-know-you-can-do-better speech. "So. I imagine you're aware how serious these violations are."

I wasn't, but I didn't want to let on so I cleverly allowed all the blood to drain from my face.

"I did some homework after our little meeting the other day. No food handler's licence. No CPR training. Flu, polio, malaria vaccinations: not up to date. No record whatsoever of any training in senior care, bereavement counselling, or public speaking." She shrugged. "Frankly, it's not looking good for Almost Family."

I pictured Dad with his eye patch flipped up, wolfing down a bowl of stale Frooty Zeros before heading out for another night at Pirate Ned's Brewery Tours.

We were toast. Burnt, margarine-smeared, way-past-the-best-before-date toast. I gulped.

"I'm sorry, but you can see what I'm up against. With this number of violations . . ." She wrinkled her nose and shook her head.

The guy came with our order. Albertina threw her hand out to stop him. "Careful! The boy hasn't had his shots. Just leave his drink on the table and step away."

The guy scurried back to the counter and started scrubbing his hands. Two girls who'd come in to check out the muffin selection turned around and left.

Albertina poured out a pile of pills and washed them down with her iced tea. "Now, Cam. I like you. Don't know why, but I do. Might be the way that in some lights, it's hard to tell if you're a boy or a girl. Kind of sweet. 'Course, I've always had a soft spot for Bloat too. So I don't want to throw the book at you fellas. Unfortunately, it's not up to me."

She took out another pill and put it under her tongue.

"But I think I may have a solution. I could use an assistant. Been begging for one for years. You help me out and I'll keep my mouth shut for a while. That should give you a chance to get your certifications up to snuff. Whaddya say?"

"What kind of assistant?"

"Oh, you know. Someone to help with my hair and makeup. Personal grooming. That type of thing."

Looked like Dad was going to have to get his Velcro parrot out of storage after all.

"Just kidding. Ha! Good Lord, you're gullible. And in case you're wondering, I do this all myself. Got a bit of a knack for it." She checked her reflection in the window, then turned back to me.

"What I actually need you for is investigative work. I'm a scam-buster. Specialty: seniors. Sad to say, but it's a growing business these days. Always someone out there ready to rip off the wrinklies." She clicked her tongue in disgust.

"Truth is, I've got a pretty effective modus operandi. The scumbag takes one look at me and thinks, 'Sweet little old lady in a wheelchair? The perfect victim.' Ha! Have I got a surprise for him."

"So what do you need *me* for, then?"

"An extra set of eyes. Someone to cause a bit of a distraction occasionally. A decoy to throw the bad guys off the scent. You get the idea. Dawned on me the other day that a wet noodle of a grandson could be the perfect decoy. Naturally, I thought of you."

Naturally.

"So what I'm proposing is this: you make yourself useful and I'll help you get your papers stamped. Heck, play your cards right and we might not even need to bother Bloat about this."

The blood started gurgling back up into my face. I actually liked the sound of this. Dad always considered Almost Family acting work. I preferred to think of it as "covert ops." Danger, excitement, forces of good and evil—that's what I kept hoping for. Of course, I didn't get to see much of that at the Gordon B. Isnor Retirement Home or the SaniWipe staff picnic. Now Albertina wasn't just proposing a solution to our little problem with the health department, she was fulfilling one of my lifelong dreams.

(And, yes, I do know how pathetic that sounds.)

"Sure." I gave her a big smile.

She didn't smile back. She tilted her head and sized me up out of the corner of her eye.

"Hmm. Your enthusiasm makes me suspicious." She tapped the table with a finger, looked out the window, then looked back at me. "Think I need to test drive you first before I commit to anything. What are you doing right now?"

Albertina didn't wait for an answer. She tucked a ten-dollar bill under her iced tea and released the brakes on her wheelchair.

"All right, then. Get moving, boy. Let's see what you can do."

CHAPTER 7

Beige hair. Beige glasses. White lab coat with *Randy* stitched in blue over the pocket. The guy sure didn't look like a scam artist to me.

"Mrs. Legge." He leaned his elbows on the counter to get eye-to-eye with her and smiled. "How might we be of help today?"

"Need my prescriptions refilled."

"Oh? Which ones?"

"All of them."

"So soon?" No more Mr. Friendly Neighbourhood Pharmacist. "You were just in last week."

Albertina let out a blast of air, like *yeah, so?*

Randy stood up and folded his arms. "Mrs. Legge. We've talked about this. Those are very powerful medications. I can't be dispensing new prescriptions each time you misplace—"

"Who said anything about *me* misplacing my medications? It was him!" She swung around like she was playing Death in a bad school play and pointed a finger in my face.

I went, "Me?!"

"Well, now, isn't he just the picture of innocence? Come on, Cam. Tell Randy what you did. Come on! Tell him." Before we'd gone into the drugstore, she'd distinctly told me to keep my pie hole shut and let her do the talking.

I made various vowel sounds. "Oh . . . ah . . . I . . ."

"Oh, crikey." Albertina swatted a hand at me. She turned back to Randy. "You probably read about it in the papers, anyway."

"Read about what?" He propped his glasses on his forehead and pinched the bridge of his nose.

"'Elderly Woman Rescued from Harbour'? Front-page news last Thursday."

"I read the paper every day. I didn't see anything—"

"Oh, come now, Randal. How could you miss it? Been nipping into your supplies or something?"

"Excuse me! I—"

"Relax. Just pulling your chain."

"Mrs. Legge. I'm a busy man. I've—"

"Okay. Then here's the *Reader's Digest* version for you. At the waterfront. Grandson's phone rings. Lets go of wheelchair to answer it. So busy cooing into his girlfriend's ear, doesn't notice the boat ramp. No idea I'd

38

done a swan dive into the North Atlantic until he hears the splash."

Randy drummed his fingers on the counter. He wasn't buying it.

"It's on YouTube," she said. "By the time they got me breathing again, I had over eighteen thousand views. Can't believe you didn't see it."

"No. Oddly enough, I did not. But what does this have to do with your medications?"

"Had them with me, case my heart acted up. Lost the whole lot of them, other than the little stash I keep by my bedside. It was very upsetting. They were in my favourite purse."

"I'm sorry to hear that." Randy's face was scrunched up into a what-kind-of-moron-do-you-think-I-am emoticon. "I suggest you get in touch with your doctor and—"

"Very upsetting, indeed. In fact, just thinking about it makes me, makes me—" Albertina put her hand on her cheek. Her eyes got big and watery. She started to pant. "Oooh . . . Cam. My purse. My. My. Purse!"

She was going mauve around the lips. I grabbed her purse from the handle of her wheelchair. She was scaring me.

She started hurling face powder and Kleenex and an unbelievable amount of eye shadow onto the floor until she found a fuzzy grey pill in the bottom and put it under her tongue.

In the thirty seconds it took to happen, Randy went from prison warden to angel of mercy. He leapt over the counter, mopped her forehead, and checked her pulse. Once he was positive she'd live, he said, "I'll have those prescriptions for you in a jiffy, Mrs. Legge."

Randy gave Albertina her medicine—and me a lecture about taking better care of my grandmother—then I wheeled her out of the Professional Centre Pharmacy and onto the sidewalk.

"Boy, but we got him good, didn't we?" Albertina was laughing so hard she was going a bit mauve again. "He fell for that cockahooey story hook, line, and stinker."

I didn't find it funny. "You lied to him. You tricked the poor guy. That's not fair."

"Fair?" She clamped her hands on the wheels of her chair and hung a U-ey. "Fair?! Well, let me tell you how this works, buster, then you tell me what's fair."

I should have kept my pie hole shut.

"Some squeaky-clean pharmacist falls for an old doll's sob story, just like mine. He tells himself she's just gotten a little forgetful, so he refills her prescription even though he's not supposed to. Doesn't think a thing about it until her grandson shows up on his own one day. Says he's going to tell the police his nanny almost OD'd on all those extra drugs—unless Squeaky slips him a few sleeping pills to keep his mouth shut. Now poor Squeaky's in a pickle, isn't he? Report the blackmail and he'll have to own up to giving the old lady the meds. He could lose his licence. Better just to dish out the sleeping pills. But the grandson doesn't want sleeping pills anymore. He wants the hard stuff now."

She dropped her voice. "And that, kids, is how you go from druggist to drug dealer in one easy step! Don't try this at home. So? Still thinking it ain't fair?"

I didn't know what to think. I pushed Albertina to her car. She'd said it was parked by the fire hydrant but that's not what it looked like. More like *mating* with the fire hydrant, if you ask me.

"But what was he supposed to do?" I said. "You practically had a heart attack in front of him."

She took a big, jangly keychain out of her purse. It had about a dozen keys hanging off it, and a large gold tube of lipstick too.

"Don't have the stomach for that, kid? Well, maybe you're not the man for me. No worries. I'll find someone else." She opened the lipstick, drew on a bright-pink clown smile, then turned back to me. "Oh, and BTW, good luck with Almost Family. Shouldn't take you any more than a year or two to get your certifications."

I immediately remembered the weird bug-repellent

smell the blue Frooty Zeros gave off and the way Dad used to stare sadly out the grimy window in our old basement apartment and try to tell me he just had something in his eye.

"No, it's not that. It's . . ."

Just then, my phone rang. I went to turn it off, but Albertina said, "Take it, take it! I got to get myself into the car anyway."

I didn't recognize the number, but Dad was always forgetting to charge his cell phone and having to use someone else's. He goes full Amber Alert if I don't pick up by the third ring. I took it.

"Cam?"

Could there be a worse time for Raylene Let's-Say-Butler to call? I turned away from Albertina and hunched over the phone.

"Yup."

"You busy?"

"Not, ah, really." Just scrambling to keep my dad and me from plunging into poverty. That's all. Same old, same old.

"Wanna get together?"

"Um." Are you *kidding* me? "Yeah."

"Can you come here?"

"Sure. Where are you?" Not that it mattered. I'd chew through concrete to get there if I had to.

"Hmm. Don't know exactly. There's a statue of this bald guy? Pigeons on his head?"

Not ringing any bells. "What street?"

"The main one? Big hill. Old building."

"Oh, Winston Churchill."

"That the street?"

"No. The statue, if it's the one I'm thinking of."

"Cranky-faced? Bow tie?"

"Yeah. That's him. You're by the library."

"Oh. Oh, right. Shoulda read the sign. Can you get here in, like, half an hour or something?"

"Sure. Just let me—" The trunk of the car opened with a gates-of-hell shriek. I turned to look.

Raylene went, "Hello? . . . Hey. You still there? . . . Your phone's cutting out."

No. My phone was fine. The problem was my brain.

It cut out when I saw Albertina hurl her wheelchair into the trunk of the car, then sashay over to the driver's seat on her hind legs.

There are Victoria's Secret models who can't walk that good in heels.

Who was scamming who here?

CHAPTER 8

Somehow I managed to get my head in gear. I told Raylene I was on my way, then hung up and turned to Albertina. I didn't have time to get into the whole wheel-chair/walking thing. I had to convince her to give me another chance and then boot it all the way to the library in less than half an hour.

I got there six minutes late, and even then, I was sweating so bad that last night's pork buns were oozing out my pores like gravy.

Raylene was sitting on the ground, her back against Winston Churchill's legs. She was cleaning her glasses on the tail of her plaid shirt. If it wasn't for the silver hair, I might not have recognized her. She looked like an entirely different person with her glasses off. Kind of softer or something.

Not so scary.

Even prettier.

Which made her scary again.

She raised her hand when she saw me but didn't say hi. I raised my hand too, then sat down more or less beside her. (Mostly less. I was the balloon. She was the pin. I knew all it would take was one touch and *kaboom*.)

She put her glasses back on. She picked up an old french fry that must have fallen out of someone's lunch and tossed it to a pigeon.

"Um," she finally said. "Guess you didn't get my message. I left you a message."

I shook my head. I thought I'd heard my phone ringing while I was running over, but was in no condition to answer it.

"Sorry I made you come all this way. I would've tried again but some other guy needed to use the pay phone and I don't have a cell."

I shrugged like *no big deal*, but something about how she said it made me think that it was.

"Thing is," she said, "I had some time before you got here and nothing to do, and when you mentioned this was the library, I thought, I don't know, may as well find out who this Winston Churchill guy is. Was. Whatever."

She picked at her fingernails. "I like random facts." She didn't laugh but made a snuffling noise that was sort of close. "You know, things that just kind of *are* and you

45

have nothing to do with and you can't change even if you wanted to. I find them weirdly relaxing."

I'd never thought of facts that way before, but I kind of got it. "No decisions to make."

"Yeah. Basically."

"I bet you're one of those people who always gets the daily special at the cafeteria."

That got a little laugh.

"No. Too dangerous. Least at my school. And anyway, big decisions like that I prefer to make on my own."

"What school do you go to?"

She acted like I hadn't said anything. She squinted into the sky for a while, then went, "So. Churchill. Like I was saying. I looked him up on wiki. You probably know this already, but he was the prime minister of Britain, and when the Nazis were bombing London all to hell and everyone thought Hitler was going to win, he gave these big, you know, like, *rousing* speeches and made everyone buck up and go *no way are we going to lose to that bulgy-eyed little jerk,* and they didn't, and he became this major hero."

She looked at me and I nodded. I only sort of knew that.

"That was kind of interesting in a, like, multiple-choice sort of way, but the thing that really got me was something else. Something his father said to him in the Early Life section."

She smiled apologetically, which I should have known meant trouble. There's never a good reason to smile at someone that way.

"Apparently, little Winston was playing with his toy soldiers one day, and his dad sees him and gets all disgusted with him for, like, being a kid and playing or something, and he says, 'You're a wastrel.'"

"A wastrel."

"Yeah. Good word, eh? 'You're a wastrel and you'll never amount to anything.' His dad actually said that to his own kid."

"Harsh."

"Yeah."

"And wrong too. I mean, by the sounds of it."

"Yeah. Winston sure showed him, didn't he? Saving the free world and everything. Nowadays, it's just the pigeons who crap all over him."

That was kind of funny, but she didn't laugh. She made one of those squiggly, I'm-sorry mouths. "That's why I called you. I read that and it's like I suddenly remembered or something. All that stuff about families? Being there for each other and everything? It's . . ." She stopped and pulled her knees up to her chin. She didn't say anything for a long time.

Long enough for me to figure it out. "Are you firing me?"

"Look. Sorry. I don't want a brother. I thought I did, but I don't. Sorry. I'll pay you."

I didn't care about that. I just didn't want her to go. I liked random facts too. I liked pigeons. (Sort of.) Mostly, I liked girls with pale skinny legs who wear cut-off jeans and workboots with the laces undone.

"You don't have to pay me. You get five hours free. Which means you've got four and a half more. You may as well use them. Maybe you'll change your mind."

She stood up and slapped grass clippings off her shorts. "Why would I want four and a half more hours of you abusing me?"

A lady sitting on a park bench looked up from her Kindle and glared at me.

"Theoretically, I mean," Raylene said and glared back at her.

I got up too. If I were someone else like Alex Tawil or Lee Chagnon or one of those guys at school who actually, you know, *interact* with girls occasionally, I would have said something along the lines of "Since you're not interested in a brother, maybe we could just hang out sometime," but I wasn't, so I didn't.

I said, "Not everyone hates their family," and tried to sound like I believed it. I would have liked to have been able to give her some actual real-life examples, but all I could think of were the empty pews at Perry's funeral, the empty visiting room at the Sunrise Manor, and Suraj putting the boots to whichever one of his many brothers was irritating him at the moment.

Raylene shrugged. "I don't want to take the chance. They're like cigarettes or something."

I didn't understand.

"Families," she said.

I nodded like *oh right, now I get it,* but clearly I didn't.

"Like, you know"—she made little circles with her hand—"they're just another addiction. That's all they are. By the time you realize how crappy they make you feel, you can't break the habit and you're stuck with them for life. I mean, how else can you explain what people put themselves through? It's like coughing up a lung every morning, then lighting up another dart." She smiled, but in a sad way or maybe an embarrassed way. "Sorry. Sure I can't pay you?"

Pay me. What? To go away? A new low even for me.

"I'm sure."

She gave this little half-wave down around her waist—which was small and had a tiny black dot of a belly button that kept flashing messages to me from below her tank top—then started walking towards the sidewalk.

Someone across the street leaned on the horn. I looked up.

I looked back down.

Albertina.

Blocking both lanes of traffic. Honking again and hollering, "Cam!" now too. (When I'd begged her to take me back, I hadn't meant immediately.)

I made a U-turn and beetled off the other way. She laid on the horn, yelled louder. And then Raylene was yelling too. "Cam! That lady wants you. Cam!"

Worlds colliding. This was going to get ugly.

I walked faster. Raylene ran after me and touched my arm. I was lucky I didn't bite my tongue off when the jolt went through me.

She pointed, although by then, it wasn't necessary. Albertina had driven her car practically up onto the sidewalk with us. She leaned out the window. "You deaf or something? What's the matter with you, boy? Hop in!"

Raylene was still holding my arm and I could feel her go kind of stiff. She jutted her chin out at Albertina. "Who do you think you are, talking to him like that?"

Albertina honked (as in with her mouth, not her horn), "What? You need your girlfriend to protect you now, Cam?

"I'm not his girlfriend." Raylene was unbelievably beautiful when she was pissed. "I'm his sister."

CHAPTER 9

It was like a scene from some zombie apocalypse movie, except with fewer missing body parts and more elastic-waist pants. An army of old people were all moaning and shuffling their way across the parking lot to a "Welcome!" sign Scotch-taped to the window of a bank-rupt Bargain Buster store.

"Where are we?" Raylene whispered as we got out of the car. I shook my head. My best guess: forty-five minutes past the edge of the known universe, but I could have been wrong. I'd had trouble keeping my eye on the road. I'd sat in the back seat of the car staring at the little tufts of silver hair poking out around the headrest. I couldn't believe how lucky I'd gotten all of a sudden.

I doubt Raylene was thinking the same thing. Round about the time all the houses started having rabid dogs chained out front, she must have wondered why she'd ever stood up for me.

She obviously didn't know what she was getting into. When Albertina'd cornered us on the sidewalk, she'd insisted that *my* sister had to be *her* granddaughter. Strong-armed Raylene into the car too. By the time Raylene realized what was up, it was too late. We were on the road to Nowheresville.

Albertina had lots to say on the way there—most notably, "Used to be a crime for a boy to look at his sister like that"—but not much in the way of useful information. All she'd tell us was that we were about to meet "the famous Dr. Blaine T. Morley, Ph.D. The *Ph* stands for *phony*. Claims he can heal the sick and talk to the dead." She did that barking thing again. "Yeah, but who can't talk to the dead? It's getting them to talk back that's the hard part."

She was the world's worst driver—although, to be fair, it's got to be tough staying on the road when you can't see over the dashboard—so by the time we got to the cheesy strip mall with the welcome sign, I didn't care where we were. I was just glad my breakfast wasn't all over the windshield, or worse, the back of Raylene's head.

I didn't know if it was the drive or the sunlight bouncing off the cars in the parking lot, but Raylene looked even paler than usual. I went to apologize for getting her mixed up in this, but she said, "No, I'm actually really interested." An old lady with the posture of a candy cane hurried past us (*hurried* being, like, relative and everything). Raylene watched her as if this were some new species she'd never encountered before.

Albertina squawked for me from the front seat. She made me carry her to the wheelchair, then we joined the zombie conga line and headed towards the storefront.

Albertina paid the twenty-five-dollar-per-person entrance fee. A young guy at the door took our names and gave us numbers, then passed us along to the official greeter. She was a middle-aged lady—tall, spokesmodel-ish, a little too thrilled to see everyone. The name tag on her blue Businesswoman Barbie suit said *Candace*.

When it was our turn, she leaned down and shook Albertina's hand. "Well, hello! And who have we here?"

"I'm Albertina and these are my grandchildren, Cam and—what's the girl's name again?" She spoke in a cracked whisper. Her head trembled.

"Raylene, Granny. Don't you remember me?" Raylene put a little trying-not-to-cry quiver in her voice. If Dad had been there, he'd have hired her on the spot.

"Sorry, dear. I'm getting forgetful in my old age." Albertina smiled sadly. "It's a blessing, actually. Don't mind forgetting my troubles, not one little bit."

Candace crouched beside her. "What troubles, honey?"

"Congestive heart failure, pancreatic cancer, sluggish

duodenum. Not much works anymore. When my Eldon was alive—that was my husband, Eldon—he'd hold my hand and sing 'My Wild Irish Rose' and the pain would disappear, just like that. I'd give anything to hear his voice again . . ."

"Well, then, I'm going to do my best to make that happen!" Candace tilted her head towards her shoulder and spoke into a tiny microphone pinned to her jacket. "Damian? I've got"—she checked the ticket in Albertina's hand—"number sixty-four and her grandchildren coming up. Find them a spot right at the front for me, would you?"

Albertina gave a tearful "Thank you. Thank you," but Candace waved it away. "Dr. Blaine wants to help you, sweetheart. That's why we're here."

The undead in the back of the line were getting restless. Candace murmured a few more words of comfort then pushed us along.

Damian was wearing a blue suit too, but it must have been XXXL, and even then, it was straining at the armpits. He removed one of the folding chairs in the front row to make room for Albertina's wheelchair, then sat us on either side.

The place looked almost as pitiful as the audience. There was a big shiny bus-sized banner of Dr. Blaine pinned on the wall ("Your lifeline to the afterlife!") but all around it, you could see grimy outlines from where the shelves used to be.

Albertina kept the bobblehead thing going but dropped the little old lady voice. "Cam," she whispered. "Get your phone out." Then, "Not like that!" She somehow managed to shriek without actually raising her voice. "What is it about the word *undercover* you don't understand? Are you *trying* to get us kicked out? For Pete's sake! Don't let them see the jeezly phone . . ." Big sigh. "Okay. Now start rolling when they call me up."

"Call you up where?"

She hissed at me to shut it. Someone had turned the music on. People quieted down. Dr. Blaine strode out of the broom closet like he was walking onto the stage in Vegas. Damian began to clap, so everyone else did too. Dr. Blaine shook his head as if he couldn't believe the spontaneous outpouring of adoration.

I could understand his surprise. He didn't look like the type of guy crowds go crazy for. Pretty much looked like every other middle-aged man, only shorter and with a nastier toupée.

I'd been to my share of funerals, so Dr. Blaine's routine was kind of familiar. He'd look all happy to have everyone there and then all sad to see so much suffering. Then he'd look up at the sky—or, in this case, the stains on the Bargain Buster ceiling—and put on one of those blissed-out, just-got-into-a-hot-bath smiles and talk about . . . I had no idea what he was talking about. I'd zoned out. I had other things on my mind.

Raylene was staring at Dr. Blaine like she couldn't believe her eyes. I was staring at Raylene like I couldn't believe mine. Who was she? What was she doing here? Like, here with me, but also here in this universe. I tried to do that Suraj thing but I wasn't very good at it.

Probably-smells-lemony.

Skin-is-very-soft.

Has-long-fingers.

Skin-is-like-*extremely*-soft.

That's the type of thinking that can get a boy in trouble, especially in public. I made myself concentrate on what was going on up front.

Dr. Blaine went, "But enough with the introductions! Our friends in the Hereafter are begging me to shut my mouth. 'Dr. B,' they're saying, 'please! Let us talk!'"

The room got all buzzy, everyone whispering and laughing and reaching out to squeeze each other's hands.

Dr. Blaine looked up at the ceiling again, then nodded as if the fluorescent light fixture had just said something to him. He turned back to the audience.

"Oh, dear. There's one spirit in particular who's being very insistent. She's pushed her way right to the front of the line. Well, you know what I say—ladies first!"

He stopped again to listen to what else she, by which I mean the light fixture, had to say.

"She's asking me to reach out to the man she calls the love of her life . . ."

More nervous titters.

". . . her knight in shining armour . . . her Pookie-Bear."

There was a squawk at the other end of the front row.

Dr. Blaine looked over. "Is that you, sir? Are you the Walter I've heard so much about?"

I got to hand it to Dr. Blaine. He didn't blink an eye when an old man about the size of a garden gnome stood up.

A couple of guys in blue suits helped Walter over to the mic. People were slapping their hands onto their chests and whispering to their neighbours. I saw a couple of ladies get out their hankies.

"I *knew* she was here." It might just have been all the emotion, but Walter sounded like he'd been sucking on a helium balloon. "Could've sworn I'd smelled her perfume the moment I walked in."

"You miss her, don't you, Walter?"

Albertina whispered, "Attaboy, Blaine. Stick the knife into the poor sucker, why don't you." She was like a ventriloquist dummy or something. Stuff came out her mouth but the blank look on her face never changed.

57

"Oh, I miss her more than I could say." Walter hung his head and began to cry.

I expected Albertina to mumble something like, "Oh, buck up, for Pete's sake," but she just went "awwww" like everyone else and didn't give me any reason not to believe she meant it.

"Well, Walt—mind if I call you Walt? I just can't bring myself to call you Pookie-Bear."

The audience loved that.

"I've got some good news for you. Shirley misses you too. In fact, there's something she's been wanting to tell you for over twenty years."

Walt kind of jolted up. "What? What?"

Dr. Blaine chuckled. "Oh, now, Walter. You know Shirley. She's a lady! She doesn't want me saying that type of thing in front of a big crowd like this. I'm almost embarrassed to tell you myself. Here, let me just turn off my mic and I'll whisper it to you."

It took two tries—apparently Walt only had one good ear—but Shirley's message made it through. Walt's eyes got bigger and bigger, his jaw bounced up and down, then he fell to the floor in a dead faint.

"The power of the spirit!" Dr. Blaine threw his arms up in the air. (I guess that's what passes for a touchdown in this business.) The crowd went crazy. Damian and his crew got Walter by the arms and legs and dragged him over to the side of the room for a little CPR.

As soon as the audience quieted down, Dr. Blaine started up again.

"Isn't that beautiful?" he said. "Do you need any more proof? Love truly knows no bounds, certainly not the whisper-thin membrane separating us from the spirit world. Only mortal constraints keep you from touching your soulmates in the Great Hereafter. That's why it's so important to help us continue our work at Dr. Blaine T. Morley Institute of Everlasting Love."

"Oh, boy. Here it comes." Albertina's little dummy face just kept smiling creepily away.

"While I take a moment to regain my spiritual strength, my associates will be passing a collection plate. Please give to the best of your abilities in order to ensure you never lose the precious bond with your family . . . your loved ones . . . your own true kindred spirits."

He bowed his head humbly, then retreated into the broom closet.

"Can you believe this guy?" I said.

I figured Raylene would be cracking up at this, but she was just staring at her lap, pulling at the frayed edge of her cut-off jeans.

"I can, actually." She looked at me. The little green

stripe in her right eye caught the light. "That's the sad thing. I'm not surprised at all. People never—"

"Shh! Not so loud. You trying to blow this or what?" Apparently, it was okay for Albertina to make comments but not for us.

The plate came by. Raylene found an old breath mint in her pocket and tossed it in. I put in sixty cents. Albertina took seventy-five bucks *out* of the collection for herself, then passed the plate on to the next guy in line.

After about five minutes, during which time I couldn't get a single word out of Raylene, Dr. Blaine reappeared at the front of the room.

"Oh, my, my. No rest for the weary! I would have loved to take more of a break, but the spirits are having none of that. It's like Lonely Hearts Night in heaven. Everyone's all gussied up on the other side and chomping at the bit to have a chat with you folks. So let's get on with it, shall we?"

Dr. Blaine put his hand on his forehead and squeezed his eyes shut as if he was thinking really hard or was severely constipated.

"The spirits are telling me there's an Alberta . . . no, sorry, an *Albertina* in the house. If you're here, please make yourself known."

Albertina elbowed me, then raised her hand, all shaky. She put on her little old lady voice again. "Why. Why. Here I am!"

60

"The spirits never fail us!" Dr. Blaine swung his arm towards her like he was a magician who'd just abracadabraed some poor rabbit out of a hat. Wild applause. Then Damian wheeled her to the front, just like Albertina said he'd do.

I propped my phone up beside me on the chair and hit record. Cam Redden, 007. This was almost too good.

Albertina was beaming up at Dr. Blaine. There was a teeny-tiny little banana cream pie of spit at the corner of her mouth. A nice touch. "What else are the spirits telling you?" Her enthusiasm would have been heartbreaking if you didn't know it was totally fake.

He held his hand to his temple again, like the play-by-play guy at a football game trying to hear his earphones. He frowned. "They're saying you're not well."

"No, I'm not."

"Is it . . ."—checking his messages again—"heart failure? And . . . and . . . cancer? Pancreatic cancer, perhaps?"

Albertina's eyes went wide. "Why, yes. Yes, it is!"

Even wilder applause. She may be dying, but *Yay for Dr. Blaine!* He got another answer right.

"However did you know that?" Albertina asked.

"It's not me. It's our friends on the other side." All Mr. Humble now. "One of them wants to make contact with you. Someone special. Did you perhaps know . . . an Eldon?"

61

She slapped her cheek. "What's he saying?"

Dr. Blaine chuckled. "He's not saying. He's singing, honey. He's singing 'My Wild Irish Rose.'"

"Sorry?" Albertina wrinkled up her face in confusion. "I missed that. Can you come a little closer?"

Dr. Blaine leaned down. "He's singing 'My Wild I—'"

Before he could get the next word out, Albertina had him in a headlock. She sent his toupée flying and yanked out his earphone.

"Eldon, my ass!" She waved the earphone in the air and turned to the crowd. "He's not talking to the dead, folks! He's talking to Candace. She's telling him what to say!"

Albertina managed to get all that out while maintaining the headlock *and* simultaneously fighting Damian off. When he got a little too close, she threw the earphone to Raylene, who jumped up on her seat and started shouting too.

"Dr. Blaine's a fraud! This is a scam!"

Damian ditched Dr. Blaine and went after Raylene. Every time he almost had her, she'd toss the earphone to me, then he'd lunge my way and I'd toss them back to her. It was like Monkey in the Middle, only played with an angry gorilla.

And a beautiful girl.

A beautiful, laughing girl.

Some of the spryer folks in the crowd were standing up to get a look at what was happening. Others had their hands cupped behind their ears and were going, "Eh? What? What's all the shouting about?"

Then, suddenly, more guys in blue suits materialized from the sidelines. They got me by the collar and Raylene by the armpits and started dragging us out, kicking and screaming. I was scared out of my mind and my heart was pounding like crazy, but mostly I was just loving it.

Damian was speeding Albertina towards the exit, but she wasn't going quietly either. She was stretched over the arm of her wheelchair like a dog with its head out a car window, hollering, "Old ain't stupid! Old ain't stupid!"

By the time security pried Raylene's fingers off the front door and manhandled us into the parking lot, the chant had caught on and the geezers were mobbing Candace for their refunds.

Best gig ever—and I'm including the time that guy took us bungee jumping.

CHAPTER 10

The thing with the toupée was hilarious.

Albertina yanked it off and it went flying and hit this lady two rows back, who totally freaked. You'd swear she was being attacked by some vicious longhaired bat. We played the video over and over again until Albertina's laughing turned into choking. Then Raylene and I ran around her little apartment trying to find pills and juice and a glass clean enough to put it in.

That was harder than it sounds. From the outside, Albertina's apartment building didn't look that bad. Just one of those brick cubes you see all over the place but nobody you know ever lives in. Her parking space was right by the back door, and the back door was right by the elevator, and the elevator opened right by her apartment.

The inside of her place was a different story. She lived in a bachelor apartment roughly the size of an SUV, so you'd think everything would be more or less nearby. Maybe it was, but that didn't mean it was easy to find.

Every square inch of the place—the porta-potty-sized bathroom, the rusty lawn chair, the TV dinner table, the itty-bitty Fisher-Price kitchen—was covered in big, fat file folders, all spewing paper and photos and old newspaper clippings. The only thing missing from the picture was a couple dozen feral cats.

Albertina managed to get a pill down and some colour back in her face. "You know, I wouldn't mind dying laughing." She wiped her nose on her wrist. "Especially if I could come back to Dr. Blaine and rub it in his face."

Raylene found a corner of a chair to sit on. "How'd you even find out about him?"

"That's my job, sugar. I'm always sniffing around trying to figure out where the bad smell is coming from."

Raylene picked up the file she'd been using as a footrest and started flipping through it. "These all people you're going after?"

"No. Most I got already. I just hang on to the evidence. Scammers are worse than cockroaches. Can never be sure they're gone for good."

I peeked in another file. I hoped there might be some random facts in there that would attract Raylene's interest. "Who's Charles Butler?"

"Charlie Butler." Albertina chuckled affectionately. "a.k.a. Craig Butler, Chase Benson, Chuck Bogdanovich. Immigration specialist—as in he specialized in ripping off immigrants. He fell for my little Russian babushka act and now he's doing twelve to fifteen for fraud."

"Brenda Anselm?" Raylene was tilting her head back and forth checking out a photo. "She looks kind of like the lunchroom monitor we had when I was little."

Albertina closed one eye and thought about it. "Don't recall. What do my notes say?"

Raylene tried to make out what she'd written. "St. Luke's *something something* dinner *something*—then maybe *saliva?* No. *Salvation?*"

"Oh, yeah. Salvation Army. Big do-gooder. Always organizing church suppers and bingos and what-have-you. And why wouldn't she? She was pocketing half the cash."

Albertina pried off a shoe. "You'd think she could have used some of it to buy herself a decent outfit. These women who let themselves go. Never understood it."

"And who's this?" I found an old black-and-white photo propped up near her bed. It was of a guy wearing a Stetson, a cowboy shirt, and one of those ties that looks like a shoelace.

"Eldon."

"There really is an Eldon?" Raylene was right beside me in a second, almost touching me, smelling more like pound cake than lemons. I love pound cake. I never knew how much I loved pound cake.

"You really are newbies, aren't you?" Albertina snorted. "Okay, undercover lesson numero uno: whenever possible, resort to the truth. The more lies you tell, the more you're likely to forget. So, yes. There really is an Eldon, or at least was. And let me tell you, I'd have been over the moon had Dr. Blaine gotten him to sing to me. No sweeter man on the face of this earth."

"What happened to him?" Raylene was braver than me.

Albertina removed her hair and put it on the TV table beside her. I tried to look as *whatever* as possible but it wasn't easy. Her head was weirdly round and almost totally bald. It looked like a white dog had randomly shed on it.

"Life," she said. "Life happened to him. It happens to all of us, of course. Some people just handle it better than others."

Raylene and I both started doing that too-happy, let's-change-the-subject thing.

"Oh, hey, and what's inside this?" Raylene moved a bunch of files off a black metal cabinet.

Albertina gave a Wicked-Witch-of-the-West shriek, which, under the circumstances, was oddly reassuring. "Don't touch that!"

Raylene jumped back. "Sorry. What is it?"

Albertina huffed, then began jimmying off the other

67

shoe. "Just the most precious thing in the world to me. My makeup kit."

Raylene and I both laughed.

"What?" Albertina said.

"Your makeup kit?" I said. "Who needs a makeup kit the size of a bar fridge?"

"Well, believe it or not, I don't wake up looking this good. Takes a few artificial ingredients these days . . ."

"Yeah, but this thing's huge."

"Are you *trying* to make me feel bad?"

Albertina glared at me. Raylene glared at me. I dropped it.

"Speaking of makeup, Raylene, why don't you let me see if I can do something with you one of these days? With a little lipstick and a lot of eye shadow, you might not be half bad."

We both laughed at that, but apparently Albertina wasn't joking.

"You'd have to lose the glasses too, of course. Which reminds me, there's a place I want to visit tomorrow afternoon and I could use some backup. You in?"

I looked at Raylene. "Yeah," she said as if the answer was obvious.

"Okay. Meet me at my doctor's office tomorrow at two. Spring Garden Professional Centre. Suite 423.

Then we'll head over. This is the big one, guys—the one that counts—so be prepared."

I didn't know what that meant, but I liked the sound of it.

She hit a lever and her wheelchair's footrest sprang up. "But, now, you can get the hell out of here, if you don't mind. I got things to do." She closed her eyes and stretched out. If she'd had a tag on her toe, you'd have thought she was dead.

"And, Cam," she said without opening her eyes, "make sure you walk that girl home. Don't want her family worrying. Lot of bad people out there."

CHAPTER 11

We'd been running Almost Family for five years. You'd think I'd have been good at this sort of thing by then, but I wasn't. When Dad realized the acting gene had skipped a generation, he came up with workarounds for me. We had a leg cast I could slap on if I was supposed to be athletic, an arm cast if I was supposed to be artistic, and a makeup kit to fake any other injury necessary to hide my total lack of talent.

Usually, though, we didn't have to resort to that. I figured out pretty fast the best disguise is just keeping my mouth shut. Don't say anything at a funeral and people assume you're too broken up to talk. Don't say anything when you're supposedly the long-lost nephew from Bulgaria and they assume you don't speak English. Go quiet anywhere else and they just figure you're a normal hormonal teenager.

In a way, Albertina had been right. Cam was short for chameleon, or should have been. I could fade into the background with the best of them.

That wasn't going to work here. It was only the two of us, walking down a dark street. I had to say something, especially since Raylene didn't look like she was going to.

"So." I was doing my best to bring my voice down below Smurfette range. "Where do you live?"

Raylene waved vaguely in front of us. She shrugged. I shrugged. I tried to smile but I felt like I'd just bought a brand-new face and wasn't sure which muscle moved which part yet.

"So"—it took me a while to get up the guts to try again—"what do you think of Albertina?"

"I like her." Raylene pulled a leaf off a tree and the branch sprang up. Little yellow things sprinkled all over us. "She's tough. She's funny. She's honest."

"Not that honest," I said. "She can walk, you know. She doesn't need the wheelchair."

"Yeah, so? Who cares about that kind of honest? I mean, you were surprised? One look at Albertina and you must have known the hair's not real."

(Actually, I didn't, at least not until it was sitting beside her.)

"Or the eyelashes. Or the boobs."

"The boobs?"

"They're hers, but they've clearly got a lot of help. Old ladies' boobs don't go straight out like that."

"Oh, right." I really didn't want to think about old ladies' boobs too much.

"The obvious stuff like that doesn't bother me," Raylene said. "Makes her happy, who cares? It's the people who pretend to be all honest and aren't that I can't stand."

"You wouldn't like many of our customers, then." I thought that might make her smile, but she'd gone back to being the old Raylene. She blew some yellow things off her shirt and looked away.

I couldn't think of anything else to say. We kept walking, not talking. I was relieved when my phone buzzed. It was just a text from Dad reminding me we had Dalton the next day, but it gave me something to do. I texted "I know" and put the phone back in my pocket.

"We got a gig tomorrow," I said, which I erroneously believed sounded cool until Raylene said, "You play music?" as if I might actually be interesting, and I had to say, "No, I mean, like, Almost Family."

She said, "You call those *gigs*?"

"Dad does." Like *can you believe it*? "But he's an actor. That's how we got into the business."

"You like it?"

"Could be worse."

"Your whole family do it?"

"Yeah," I said.

"Even your mother?"

I forgot about her. "No. I haven't seen my mother in years."

Raylene stopped and looked at me as if she'd missed something before. She didn't say sorry. Guidance counsellors always do when they find out. They usually hug me too, before they send me back to class. I was hoping Raylene would hug me, but she didn't.

"So it's just you and your dad?"

"No. There are other people who work for us too, but you mean relatives? Then, yeah. It's just us. What about your family?"

"I met you when I tried to rent a brother. Kind of says everything you need to know."

"Need to? Well, I guess." I tried to get some spit back into my mouth. "But I'm like you."

She smiled a little, one eyebrow up. "Meaning . . . ?"

"I like random facts too."

Now both eyebrows were up and it was a real smile.

"I'd like to know some random facts about you," I said, my heart jackhammering away at my molars. "If you don't mind."

"So polite." She folded the leaf down the centre and threw it like a paper airplane. "Okay. Five-foot-six. Ish. Allergic to melons. Pet peeve: long toenails."

"On you or someone else?"

"Someone else. I can control my own toenails."

"Like, telekinetically or something?"

I made her laugh. She hit me.

"As in, clip them. But seriously, that really bugs me, and it's not just a grooming thing either. I've always thought there was something creepy and, I don't know, *prehensile* or whatever about long toenails. I'm suspicious of people who have them."

"Because they might use them to suddenly start scrambling up trees or something?"

She stopped and looked at me, all kind of twinkly, so I boldly carried on. "And then their jackets would tear open and hair would sprout all over the place?"

"Yes." She flapped her hands out to the side. "Yes. Exactly. I'm not saying they *would* but that's certainly the impression they give. I mean, in this day and age, what civilized human being needs toe claws? I never understood why other people can't see that. They're like, *Oh, So-and-so just couldn't find the nail clippers*, and I'm like, *No. It's way weirder than that*."

"Makes perfect sense to me." Sorta, now that she mentioned it. "It's like in the movies. You know, those ones where the only way you can tell the aliens from the humans is by whether they have a functioning belly button or not."

"Functioning." Another little laugh from her. "You

know, it actually *would* kind of make a good movie."

I thought that was just one of those *yeah-yeah-sure* lines people use when things get awkward, but then she went, "It could open on a couple at a fancy restaurant. Man pours the lady some wine. She does that sexy-face thing and he's all *hey-hey-hey*—but under the table, you see her perfectly polished toenails ripping through her Manolo Blahniks."

"Which I'm almost positive are shoes of some type."

"Clever boy."

I tried not to love that too much. "Or what about a bus driver?"

"Interesting."

"He'd be laughing and joking with the little kids as they all pile on with their little novelty backpacks and missing teeth and everything. Then he'd close the door. Pull onto the road. And the camera would zoom down on his foot hitting the accelerator—"

". . . and a single gnarly claw . . ."

"Yup. Tears right through his boots."

"Brilliant. Children in peril. A must for the modern slasher film."

"The possibilities are kind of endless." This was weirdly almost like talking with Suraj. As long as I didn't let myself think about how she looked, sounded, or smelled, my brain seemed to function just fine.

I said, "The Queen waving from the porch at Buckingham Palace . . ."

"I doubt the Queen calls that the porch."

"You know what I mean."

"A surgeon with those little green booties they wear in the operating room . . ."

"Good one . . . Santa's elves with the curly slippers . . ."

"Oooh. Ick. Ick." She waved her hands around and scrunched her eyes closed. "You'd need really long toe-nails for that. Ooh. And they'd have to bend backwards too. Ick."

"Sorry. Too much?"

"Yes." Gag face. "Can we change the subject?"

"Sure," I said, because, by now, I'd firmly established myself as a ladies' man. "Let's talk about your family."

She mouthed *ha-ha*. "Shouldn't you know every-thing already? Aren't you supposed to be my brother?"

"Not anymore. Your five free hours are up. C'mon. I told you about my sorry excuse for a family. You should tell me about yours. Fair's fair."

She considered that. "Agreed—but I can't right now because there's a gas station just across the street and I really need to pee."

"Another random fact about you!" I said. She walked away laughing. The light from the gas station lit up her hair like a halo.

I waited outside. Dad texted again, wanting to know my ETA. I answered, "Two hours." I was making headway and wasn't going to blow it.

He texted back "one hour" and a long list of articles of clothing that had to be lint-brushed for tomorrow. (Dalton is our best customer. Dad always gets wound up before Dalton.)

I texted "1.5" but wondered if that would be enough. Raylene was taking forever. I hoped that was a good sign. Maybe she was freshening up—brushing her teeth, mussing her hair, whatever it is girls do when they're out with a hot guy.

I went into the gas station and bought some Mentos. I figured my breath could stand a little freshening up too. I noticed the door to the ladies' room was open. I looked around the store. Raylene wasn't there.

I turned to the counter guy. "Um, you see a girl with, like, silver hair? Came in to use the washroom?"

"Yeah. She left ages ago." He handed me my change. "Asked if she could sneak out the back door. Said some creep wouldn't leave her alone."

CHAPTER 12

It was closing time and Suraj was cleaning out the meat case when I got to the deli. He made me a sandwich from some green pastrami he found stuck to the bottom. I wolfed it back. With any luck, it would kill me and I wouldn't suffer anymore.

He had to watch the toupée video several times before he could get a handle on Albertina. ("The-Joker-in-drag." It wasn't his best, but it did kind of capture that whole unhinged vibe she gave off.)

He'd finished up the cash before I could bring myself to tell him about what happened with Raylene. He had an entirely different take on it than I did.

"So she called you a creep. You ask me, that's a step up. Remember Ariana Lidgate? You, like, *stalked* her for six months straight and she still had to ask your name when she signed your yearbook. At least Raylene noticed you. Now we just have to work on your presentation."

What did it say about my life that I needed presentation tips from a guy wearing a paper hat and a whisker net?

"But I wasn't being a creep. That's the thing."

"How do you know?"

"I just know. She laughed. She smiled. She actually hit me!"

"She hit you. And you don't think she thought you were a creep."

"No. Not hit me like *leave me alone*. Hit me like *you're funny. You're cute.* Girls do that all the time."

"You're telling me. I am positively covered in bruises."

"I really thought she liked me."

"Here. Eat your heart out." He pushed an almost empty bowl of guacamole across the counter and a handful of broken pita chips. "The way I see it is, there are girls and then there's warrior-princess-from-an-HBO-fantasy-series. I think you're aiming too high. Better just stick with girls for a while. Maybe Lynette What's-Her-Face has a niece or something."

I nodded and tried to avoid the guacamole scabs crusting up the edge of the bowl. He was probably right.

CHAPTER 13

You can say a lot of things about Dalton, but at least he's got style. The limo was there to pick us up by eight the next morning. There were fresh pastries and orange juice spread out on a table between us and new games uploaded onto the computer.

We were both cranky. Dad because he was cutting down on coffee. Me because—well, nothing like getting called a creep to make you want to alienate the only person alive who truly loves you.

It takes about an hour to get to the prison. We stuffed our faces for a while, then started kind of half-heartedly playing *Rage of Gnorr*.

Dad cornered a bunch of my mercenaries in an underwater cave and said, "By the way, we have Sharon tonight."

I groaned. Sharon was The Absolute Worst.

"I'm busy," I said and aimed wildly at his guy. I missed.

"I know you are. You're going to Sharon's event with me."

"Dad. Have a heart! Can't you find someone else?" I was so mad I could barely figure out whose men were whose anymore.

"No. You're her son. She's had you for years. It would look weird to change. How would she explain someone new to her friends?"

"What friends?" I said. By this time, I only had three footmen left and either Dad or that sharky thing was going to get them pretty soon.

"The mere fact you have to ask is reason enough to go. Plus she likes you."

I gagged. "It's so creepy."

"What? Someone liking you? Don't be so hard on yourself. You're not that bad. I mean, *usually*."

"Oh my God. I can't believe you actually think you're funny."

He put on his best Arnold Schwarzenegger sneer and obliterated the last of my men. "And you thought denying me caffeine vould stop me!" He was using the accent now too.

"That doesn't count." I winged my controller at him.

"Does too."

"Does not. You can't hit me with the news that I have to see Sharon tonight, then use my despair as a chance to kill my entire army. That's cheating. I want a do-over."

"Psychological warfare is totally legit. This isn't child's play, you know."

"Fine. Then I'm not going with Sharon."

"Fine, then we'll have the do-over. I suppose you want me to use my left hand this time too."

I did.

"No, I just want you to play fair. What depressing hellhole is she taking us to this time anyway?"

Dad took another croissant and piled jam on it. Bad sign. His inner fat boy always turned to sugar when he got nervous.

"Where?" I squinted at him. He pretended not to notice.

"Some little fundraising do."

More jam.

"What kind of fundraiser?"

"At the trampoline park. It'll be fun!"

"No. You are not *seriously* using one of Bloater's lines on me, are you? 'It'll be *fun!*' That's exactly the type of thing he'd say right before some big very-not-fun disaster hit. This is not amusing, Dad. I mean it."

"Okay. Fine. Adolescent suicide prevention."

I banged my head against the window and fake-cried. "Do you have any idea how painful this is going to be? You know what? I'll tell you the best way to prevent at least one teen suicide: don't make me go."

Dad went quiet. Like, dead quiet.

"Don't you *ever*—I mean, *ever*—let me hear you say that again, Cam. Understand?"

"Chill. I was only joking."

"Well, don't."

He ate another Danish.

After a while, he threw me back my controller. "Time for your do-over. And don't expect me to take it easy on you just because you're being a wimp."

But he did. It's the only possible way to explain how I won the next three games.

CHAPTER 14

Over the years, I've gotten to know the guards, so even though frisking still isn't great, they do at least let me know when to brace myself. McInerney always whistles at the fancy suit Dad's wearing and makes a big deal about checking the label. (Another good thing about Dalton: he gives us a clothing allowance.) Depending on the time of year, Whitton always asks how my hockey, soccer, or basketball season's going. He's apparently under the delusion I'm some kind of athletic prodigy, my total lack of muscle mass notwithstanding. I just shrug and smile and try to look humble. We have to take off our fancy watches and pinky rings, then we're led into the visitor's room.

Dalton was in his usual fine form that day. Hearty smile. Backslap for Dad. Fake one-two punch for me. He used to be a lawyer with a big house on the water and a bigger one down south until the cops figured out he'd been stealing from his clients to pay for them. The houses were the first to go. The wife, kids, and grandkids went pretty soon after. If it weren't for us, no one would visit him.

It doesn't seem to get him down. "I paid through the nose for their love and affection, and look where it got me. At least with you guys, it's an up-and-up business deal."

And here's the deal:

a) We—i.e., his adoring son and grandson—make him look like he's still The Man in front of his jailhouse peeps.

b) He pays us.

No script, no names, no places to remember. All we have to do is act rich, which in my case just means showing up in the clothes he picked out for me. Piece of cake. Eight more years of his sentence, several visits a month—I'm thinking it'll see me through university.

As long as there's no guard listening, we can talk about anything we want. That day, Dad needed legal advice. There was some guy refusing to pay because the great-uncle he'd rented couldn't remember anyone's names. (Seemed unfair to us. Frank's pushing ninety! He's a bit hazy on anything that's happened since 1945. Dad thought it gave a nice note of realism.)

There's nothing Dalton loves more than showing how much he knows. He started quoting laws and statutes and what I can only presume was the Monopoly rule book, and normally I would have zoned out, but it got me thinking. About Albertina. If anyone could find an easy way around all the regulations we were breaking, it would be Dalton.

I waited until Dad went to get some pop from the machine, then I asked. (Dad always makes sure to give me a little quality alone time with "Papa D.")

Dalton looked at me like I'd lost my mind.

"Why would you need malaria vaccinations or a food handler's licence?" He had a good guffaw over that one. "That Albertina broad is scamming you, son! You guys are just acting. That's all you're doing. You don't need any certification for that. If you did, The Rock would still be manning a parking booth in Waikiki."

Dad came back with two root beers and a Diet Coke. He patted me on the back and smiled. He was pleased I'd made Dalton laugh.

CHAPTER 15

It had been a crappy couple of days. First the Raylene thing. Next finding out about the gig with Sharon. And now Albertina.

I mean, *Albertina*? Actually scamming *me*?

Something snapped. Yes, outing Dr. Blaine was the most fun I'd had in ages, by which I mean my life, but it didn't matter. I was done. Finished. I was only going to the doctor's office because I wanted to give her a piece of my mind. Maybe make a bit of a scene myself. See how she liked it.

I got to the waiting room about five to two. "You're early," Raylene said. "She's still with the doctor."

My mouth opened and then just kind of hung there, helplessly, like Suraj on a chin-up bar or something. What was *Raylene* doing here?

She patted the chair next to her and said, "Sit."

I sat. She bumped me with her shoulder. "Sorry about last night."

"What, like, happened?"

"It was time to go." Cutesy grimace. "So I left. Sorry."

Oh, right. Good answer. I didn't know whether to be mad she'd taken off then or glad she was here now. I settled for angry but confused. We flipped through separate copies of *Urinary Tracts Today!* or whatever the stupid magazine was called and waited for Albertina.

The doctor wheeled her out the door. Raylene popped up. "Granny!"

"So these are the grandchildren I've heard so much about." The doctor shook our hands. "Clive Ewan." He was a beefy guy with a shaved head and a full beard. I wouldn't have been surprised if he had a Hells Angels patch sewn on to the back of his white lab coat, but he seemed nice enough.

"Listen," he sort of whispered while Albertina was fiddling with something in her purse. "I understand you'll be seeing your older sister later. Do you think we could all get together for a little chat about your grandmother's care? I'd be happier if we could get her into some type of—"

Albertina slammed her purse shut. "Who cares if *you're* happy? I'm fine. They're busy. See ya." She started pushing herself towards the door.

He looked at us. "If you ever need to talk, just—"

"I said I'm leaving. Now move it, kids!"

Dr. Ewan sighed and scratched his ear. I bit my lip, as in *Sorry,* then we left.

Albertina was waiting by the elevator, steaming. "The older you get, the more they treat you like a baby. Trust me. That's the last time I'm letting that guy look under *my* johnny shirt."

She fumed all the way down to the lobby and I chickened out. I couldn't tell her off now. She was scary enough when she was in a good mood.

Or maybe Albertina had nothing to do with me keeping my mouth shut about the scam. Raylene smelled as goddess-like as ever, even if she had been a dick. I knew I'd probably regret it—I wasn't stupid—but I wanted to hang around. I just had to figure out a way to do it without looking pathetic.

The elevator door opened. Albertina told me the car was parked in the same spot as yesterday. Said she'd meet us there in a couple of minutes—she had something she needed to do. She headed one way. We headed the other.

This time it was Raylene trying to make conversation with me. "I wonder what the doctor wanted to talk to us about."

I shrugged. Once bitten and all that.

"Weird she told him about us, eh? Albertina only just met me."

I leaned against the car and crossed my ankles. "She told him about *somebody*. Doubt it had anything to do with us or our . . . older sister." I could be a dick too. I still had enough pride left for that. I turned and watched a bicyclist almost get creamed running a red light.

"Are you mad?" she said.

"Why would I be mad?" Let her fill in the blanks.

An old lady was having trouble getting down the wheelchair ramp. I went to help her. I was a dick perhaps, but at least I was a gentleman dick.

"Need a hand?"

The lady went, "Would everybody please stop treating me like I'm some jeezly double amputee!" and that's when I realized it was Albertina. No wig, no false eyelashes, skinny grey lips. She'd even traded her high heels for fuzzy slippers. She was totally unrecognizable.

She rolled down the ramp to the car. Raylene had her hands on either side of her face and was going, "Whoa. Awesome disguise!" as if Albertina's "disguise" was something she'd put on, as opposed to something she'd taken off and stuffed in her purse.

"With teeth or without?" she asked, and gave us a gummy smile.

"Without," Raylene said. "Definitely without."

We got in the car. I pretended to sulk while Albertina told us what we had to do. It was a little hard to understand her toothless, but basically she seemed to be saying we were the lead on this one. Her job was just to sit there looking senile while we pretended to be checking out an adult daycare for her. One of us had to distract the owner. The other had to snoop around the place.

"Get lots of pictures." I hadn't realized until that moment that one of the reasons people have teeth is to keep spit from spraying all over the place when they talk. "I want to know all the dirt on this gal. Where she lives. Her family. Her hobbies. Her pets. A little DNA would be nice too, but only if you can manage to get a cheek swab without arousing suspicion. When you're done, I should be able to build a life-sized replica of her from your notes."

We pulled up outside a church hall in the west end. The street was empty, which was a good thing. People generally frown on demented seniors careening at top speed through residential neighbourhoods. I took out Albertina's wheelchair and she got herself in.

The sign said "Time of Our Lives Adult Daycare" and also mentioned it didn't open until three o'clock, but that was okay—Albertina had phoned ahead to arrange a tour for her "grandmother." She laid on the buzzer. The door opened a couple seconds later.

I'd expected someone older. The girl looked like she was in her late twenties. She was wearing old-style cat's-eye glasses and clothes that seemed less *adult* than *daycare*. Puffy flowered skirt, a man's jean jacket, and a scarf tied around her head in a big floppy bow. Undiluted hipster.

"Mrs. Legge? Come in! Come in!" She held the door and we squeezed past her. "I'm just getting ready for this afternoon's session, so excuse the mess."

It didn't look that bad to me. There were chairs and tables set up in little pods. I could see art supplies at one, balls of wool at another, and board games too.

"I'm Janie Aikens. I'm the owner." She put her hand on Albertina's shoulder and smiled. "So how do you like to spend your time, Mrs. Legge? Singing? Playing cards? Baking? There's always something fun happening here." Albertina looked back blankly, wobbling her head and licking her lips with a sticky white tongue.

Janie turned to us but didn't move her hand. "It can be a bit much for first-time guests, taking it all in. Shall we go for a little stroll around the activity stations?"

Albertina pinched me hard, which was either just mean or my signal. "Mind if I use the washroom?" I squeaked. Janie must have thought I needed to go really bad.

"Not at all. It's just down the hall, one door past my office."

I had no idea what Albertina wanted, and I was suddenly so nervous at having an actual undercover job that I really did need to pee now. I slipped into the office. It was small and messy and jammed full of stuff. Drawings on the wall and thank-you cards and Post-it notes about people's allergies and medications. Tons of photos too, mostly of the old folks in Halloween costumes or Santa hats or banging on their little rhythm instruments. I got pictures of it all.

I pushed the papers around on her desk and got shots of everything there too.

I opened some drawers, but that was too much. No way I could photograph every person's file. I found one labelled "Business Documents." It seemed to have Janie's address and age and probably some other highly confidential information too, so I focused on that. I just hoped fifteen-and-a-half-year-olds couldn't be sentenced to hard labour. I'd ask Dalton about that next time.

I got up to go and noticed some photos tacked to the back of the door. There was Janie with an old chocolate Lab, Janie with some other girls at a beach, Janie with a dark-haired, bearded guy in matching hipster glasses. Lots of him. I figured that's who she must have swiped the jean jacket from. There were also a few old black-and-white photos that must have come from her family album. I got pictures of everything, then booted it back to the church hall.

Janie was telling Raylene and Albertina about membership fees. ". . . but if that's too steep, talk to us. We won't turn anyone away. We'll do our best to work something out that's fair."

Albertina was really pulling out all the stops now. She was hanging on to Janie's hand like a little kid on her first day of school. She'd even managed to produce an impressive amount of tears.

"Sure you won't stay with us today, Mrs. Legge? See if you like it here?"

"I'm sure she'd love to," Raylene said, "but we've got to get her to the hairdresser."

We both realized her mistake at the same time.

"The dentist," I said, which wasn't much better, given that he clearly wouldn't have a lot to work with.

"For me, that is. She likes to come to the dentist with me," I said. "I'm getting a root canal."

Janie smiled like *isn't that nice,* but we raced Albertina out of there so fast she must have known something was up.

CHAPTER 16

Albertina moved the car around the corner where we wouldn't be seen. "So. Spill. Get anything good in Janie's office?"

I shrugged. "Nothing that seemed very incriminating to me."

"*Pfft!* You're not suspicious enough. Give me your phone." Her hand was still damp from putting her teeth back in, and now mine was too. I thought of the necrotizing virus that kicked off Armageddon in Suraj's fifth book and hoped my fingers wouldn't dissolve before I could find a wet wipe.

"So who's this cowpoke?"

"I think that's her boyfriend." I leaned over from the back seat and showed her how to scroll. "There were lots of pictures of him."

Albertina wobbled her head. "Not a bad-looking fella, if he'd do something about that flea-bitten beard . . . She's got a dog, eh? And a house. She own it?"

How was I supposed to know?

"She plays the saxophone . . . Interesting."

"Why?" Raylene and I both said it at the same time. We were apparently in some sort of contest.

Albertina ignored us. She flipped through the rest of the photos, had a good gawk at one in particular, then tossed the camera back at me.

"Enough of this." She pulled out. "Got to fix myself up before someone catches me without my face on." She screeched through a couple of blocks until she found a Starbucks, then beetled into the restroom. She had her sweater pulled over her head like a suspect on a perp walk.

Raylene and I were stuck in the car alone.

"I wonder what that Janie's up to." Nothing like ditching me the night before to make Raylene all chipper today. "I mean, Dr. Blaine had *sleazoid* written all over him, but Janie? Didn't seem like that at all. In fact, I kind of liked her skirt. Wish I'd asked where she got it."

"So people whose clothes you like would never do anything bad." I didn't really want to be a jerk anymore. I just couldn't figure out how to stop.

"Yeah," she said. "Sure makes life a lot easier, being able to spot the good guys right off and everything."

"You're not serious. Clothes and toenails—that's how you judge people?"

She turned around and looked at me, eyes blank as a doll's. "No. I am not serious. At least about the clothes. Toenails, of course, are a different matter. Why are you so cranky?"

"I'm not." I rolled down the window.

"Are so."

"Am not."

"Okay. Fine. You're not. Whatever."

"Okay. Fine. I am. I don't like being called a creep. Guess I'm funny that way."

"The guy told you I said that? He shouldn't have told you that."

"You shouldn't have said it."

"You shouldn't have been prying into my personal life."

"Oh, so I'm prying when I ask about your family but not vice versa?"

I think she laughed, but she was facing the other way now. "Yeah, basically."

I pretended I was laughing too. I stared at the Starbucks sign and tried to figure out what was going on with the mermaid's tail. It had never made any sense to me. Did she have two? One, cut in half?

I was no further ahead when I saw Albertina walk out the door. She was all done up again in full technicolor. I'd forgotten how hard on the eyes she could be.

"So, kids, what say I take you out for cheap eats somewhere?"

Raylene opened her mouth to answer, but no way was I letting her ditch me first.

"Sorry. Can't. I'm busy this evening." I hoped it sounded like I had a hot date. Raylene didn't need to know it was with Sharon.

"Me too," she said.

I gave a little snort like *sure*.

She shook her head like *you moron*.

Then Albertina made some crack about "trouble in paradise" and I got out of the car and slammed the door.

CHAPTER 17

There were so many reasons I hated Raylene.

The way she kept ditching me. The way she acted so smart. The way she, like, idolized Albertina. The way she smelled so good.

I didn't want to have anything to do with her anymore.

That's what I was thinking when I walked into the apartment, so maybe I was a bit distracted.

Someone grabbed me from behind and said, "Don't move or I'll shoot" in a thick Russian accent.

It pissed me off. I jabbed my elbow back and went, "Dad. Quit it, would you?" I was in no mood to goof around.

"I'll shoot. I mean it."

He thought he was so funny, crouched down and acting all Mr. Paid-Assassin with that stupid can of Reddi-wip aimed at me.

I pushed it away and sort of went, "Gaah!" or "Erg!" or something.

"What are you so cranky about?" he said.

"Would everyone quit telling me I'm cranky?" I stormed into my room and slammed the door.

I kicked a bunch of dirty clothes off my bed and flopped down face-first. My bed stunk. My life stunk. I didn't know why I ever even thought I liked Raylene. I was so much happier when it had just been me and Dad and Suraj and the odd leftover hunk of mortadella.

Mortadella you could at least count on.

Dad knocked on the door. I said, "Go away," and put the pillow over my head.

He opened the door and came in.

"Dad!" I grabbed the pillow and threw it at him. I missed.

"Now now. This'll make you feel better." He had two cans of Reddi-wip. He handed me one.

I wouldn't take it. He shrugged and put it on the bedside table, then he opened his and sprayed a big swirl into his mouth.

"I know why you're upset," he said. The whipped cream made his voice sound like a boot squelching through mud or something. It was disgusting.

"No, you don't, actually."

"Yes, I do, actually. I'm not as dumb as you think."

Did Suraj tell him about Raylene? I was going to pound that little jerk.

"Sharon." He wiped some cream off his lips, then licked his fingers. "That's what's bugging you."

I almost laughed. Right. Sharon. She was the least of my problems at the moment.

"I owe you an apology. I was thinking about it today and realized how Nu Luv I'd been." That was our slang for *stunned*. If you ever saw *Up to No Good*, you'd know why. "I get kind of lost in my own little world. I was just thinking it was a gig. I wasn't thinking about its effect on you. Remember that episode about the Italian sweater?"

Of course I did. Thanks to the miracles of modern recording technology and Dad's sad obsession with *UTNG*, I practically knew every episode by heart.

I didn't say anything.

"It's the one where the boys in the band buy Bloat this really expensive sweater so he'll feel good about himself for his big date. He doesn't want it, but they badger him into wearing it even though he can barely get it on, and in the end he feels even worse about himself than he did before."

". . . until, of course, Nu Luv breaks out into their number-one hit 'Beautiful Inside' and he realizes it's his inner self that really counts blah, blah, blah."

"So you do remember it."

"Yes, I just don't know what it has to do with me. Or

care, actually." I wished he'd just go away so I could eat my Reddi-wip in peace.

"Well, I realized I'm doing the same thing to you that Nu Luv did to Bloat."

"Right. Giving me an expensive sweater would be *exactly* like making me go out with Sharon."

"What I mean is I think I'm doing something *to help you* when I'm actually—if accidentally—doing something that would hurt you."

I hated it when Dad got all emo drama-school on me. "If you start singing 'Beautiful Inside,' I'm going to puke."

"No, I'm being serious here, Cam. You've never had a mother. Or at least not a mother like most kids do. And, look, I'm to blame for that as much as anyone. Maddie could have stepped up to the plate a bit more, and I know, in her own way, she's sorry for that now. But I was the reason she left in the first place. She married me thinking I was a certain person, then I went and turned myself into a whole different one. That's not what she signed up for. So both of us have things to answer for—but you're the one who ends up paying the price. And most of the time, you're pretty darn good about it, but I think I pushed you too far with Sharon. It's one thing being someone's grandson or nephew or cousin. It's another thing for a motherless boy to have to play some mother's son. That can't be easy. 'Specially the way Sharon looks at you."

He had it so wrong.

Yes. I hated the way Sharon looked at me. Any normal kid would. But the mother thing? Big deal.

I know it sounds bad, but I really don't think about my mother at all. I barely remember her. I mean, I *remember* her. I know what she looks like and everything. And she came here a couple of years ago, so it's not like we lost touch. But I don't remember her living with us. I don't remember her actually being a mother. So what's there to miss?

And to tell the truth, I kind of agree with Raylene. Who says families are so great? If they were, Dad wouldn't have a business. (Frankly, if I'd had a choice between a mother and a dog right at that moment, I'd probably have taken the dog. Spend as much time as I do with the "flesh and bloods"—that's what Dad calls our clients—and it's hard to be sentimental.)

But I'm not an idiot. No way I was telling Dad that. I rolled over and sat up. "So does that mean I don't have to go then?"

"No. You still have to go. I'm just saying I'm sorry I signed you up for it in the first place. I owe you one. Now, here." He tossed me my can of Reddi-wip. "Give yourself a few mouthfuls and let's get going."

I made loud dangerous animal sounds until he was out the door, then I sucked back some Reddi-wip.

"And if you need help gluing that wig on, just give me a call!" He thought he was so funny. "Can't have your hair bouncing off and scaring the kiddies!"

104

CHAPTER 18

Sharon was the saddest person I ever met. Her mouth would sometimes sort of quiver up into a smile, but her eyes never did. Dad always said that's why I wasn't allowed to do anything stupid. If something happened to me, he'd be exactly like her. I couldn't do that to the world.

Sharon picked us up and we drove to High-Jinx Trampoline Park, somewhere out in the burbs. A big poster out front said, "Welcome to Bounce Back: A Fundraiser in Support of Adolescent Suicide Prevention!!!" Gee, that would have sounded really depressing if someone hadn't thought to add the three exclamation points.

"This looks like fun," Sharon said, and gave one of those little U-shaped quivers. She was wearing a brown skirt and a brown sweater and black old-lady shoes. Her glasses were around her neck. Everything about her just positively screamed, "Wheeee!"

"Yeah!" said Dad. "I love trampolines!" He didn't. "I can hardly wait to get on!" Right. Two bounces and there'd be Reddi-wip all over the walls.

We went in, and the first person we saw was Reverend Muncaster. She was taking tickets at the door.

"Sharon!"

"Carole." The Reverend was the type of minister who got called by her first name a lot. "You know my husband, Gary . . . and our son, Josh."

I could tell Reverend Muncaster was trying not to laugh. Apparently, the strawberry-blond mushroom-cut and braces did not suit me. It didn't help, either, that the clothes Sharon made me wear went out of style a good twenty years ago. I looked like an extra from *Up to No Good*, as Dad had been delighted to point out. At least the glasses hid most of my face.

"Yes, of course! Isn't this a wonderful family outing. So glad you could make it."

"Oh, wouldn't miss it." Sharon was reaching into her purse for her Kleenex, thus beating her previous record of zero to tears in thirty seconds. "A dear friend of mine lost her son to suicide a number of years ago, same age as Josh. Then her marriage broke up and well . . . I think of her all the time and count my blessings. Could just as easily have been me."

Reverend Muncaster stamped our hands, then when Sharon wasn't looking, gave my arm a little shake and whispered, "You're a saint."

We stood at the door and looked in. The gym was like one giant wall-to-wall trampoline. People were on it playing basketball and dodge ball and doing flips. Some were in goofy costumes. I have no idea why. Suicide isn't usually that festive.

"Lots of kids your age, sweetie," Sharon said. "Why don't you go on in? Dad and I will watch from the viewing stands. Is that okay, Gary? You don't mind sitting this one out, do you? I just think I'd like some company."

Dad said, "No, no. Not at all, sweetheart. Josh and I can always come back together another time."

He smiled at me, all smug and everything, and if Reverend Muncaster hadn't just said I was a saint, I probably would have done something I regretted. Instead I put on my best Gee-Whiz-Josh face and went, "Can I go now? I really want to give it a try!"

"Teenage boys." Little chuckle, or as close as Sharon ever got to one. "Go. Go. But be careful, Josh. You have a bad stomach. If you don't feel well or if there are too many kids jostling you about, we can always leave. Whenever you want. No shame in that."

I nodded and gave her a big grin. A real one. Ten

minutes bouncing. Bad stomach. Twenty minutes home. With a little luck, I'd be back by the time Suraj finished work.

I climbed onto the trampoline.

Raylene was standing at the entrance, smiling at me.

CHAPTER 19

I don't know what my face did, but it must have been something weird.

Raylene went, "Well, hello there!" Big, twinkly smile.

I panicked. "Ahh . . ." I looked away. Sharon saw me and waved from the bleachers. Dad would kill me if I blew cover. I waved back.

I stared at my sneakers and whispered, "Well, *this* is awkward. Not sure what I should do here." I figured if I looked right at Raylene, she'd pee herself laughing. Then Sharon would get upset because someone was making fun of Josh, and then there'd be more tears and Dad in a flap. Major scene. Loss of a good client. Bills not paid, etc., etc.

At least Raylene seemed to be able to control her voice. "Hmm. Well. Let's see. There are lots of choices. Basketball's at that end. Free-form bouncing over there. Dodge ball in the middle. You can do whatever you want. Any questions, just look for a volunteer. We're all wearing these orange T-shirts. Oh, and snacks are in the lobby."

I looked up. She smiled and said, "Have fun!"

No wink. No elbow nudge. No squiggly lips fighting to keep down a laugh. She clearly had no idea who I was. All I could think was thank God for ugly wigs, fake braces, and glasses the size of scuba masks.

I didn't hang around to let Raylene get a second look. I scrambled down to the other end of the trampoline. I'd escaped.

I planned to stay there until she left her post near the door and I could slip out, but I sort of drifted back. Before I could help myself, I was bouncing with a bunch of twelve-year-olds right next to her.

I kept it low-key. I didn't want Sharon shrieking (which she did every time I bounced more than six inches in the air), and I sure didn't want Raylene noticing me. I was basically lurking.

So much for never wanting to see her again.

Raylene led a bunch of little kids in some sort of musical game for a while. She held hands and bounced with a disabled guy until he got tired. Then she had a long serious talk with a lady in a Minnie Mouse costume. From what I could hear, it was mostly about volunteering and how wonderful it was to see young people doing their part, but then the lady said, "I know how difficult it must be for you. I understand your family's been touched by it too."

I didn't hear what Raylene said to that. Her back was to me, and before I could bounce around to a better spot, Dad had started calling and waving from the viewer's gallery.

He was like some demented inflatable air dancer at a second-hand car lot. He wasn't going to stop until I responded. I sighed and went over to see what he wanted.

"Your mother's getting tired, so whenever you're ready . . ."

"Ten more minutes?" I said.

He checked with Sharon. "Okay."

I turned to go back to Raylene and the Mouse Lady but they'd disappeared. I looked around the gym. No sign of them. Maybe they'd gone for a snack. I stumbled full speed across the trampoline. (In any other context, I would have found that hilarious. Try running across a floor that bounces back. Newborn giraffes look more coordinated.)

I had no idea what I was going to say to Raylene if I found her, but I *had* to find her. I wobbled off the trampoline and into the lobby. The place was jammed. People were still arriving. Others were leaving. Big kids were elbowing their way to the food table. Mothers were racing little kids to the washrooms.

I noticed Kev, one of our Almost Family freelancers, over in the corner, chowing down on a chicken wrap. He was dressed in your standard high-school biology teacher uniform—pleated chinos, button-down shirt, and novelty tie. (I'm always amazed how well he manages to cover up his neck tattoo for these gigs. Must take a pile of concealer to hide that beast.)

"Oh, hi, Mr. Dakin. Didn't expect to see you here."

Kev looked right at me but didn't give a thing away. He never breaks character. (Weird guy, but professional.)

"Oh, hey, Josh. Thought I saw your parents here. How ya doin'?"

"All right. I'm just looking for someone."

"Yeah?"

"You haven't seen a girl with silver hair, have you?"

He chewed thoughtfully, then shook his head. "Sorry."

"What about a lady in a Minnie Mouse costume?"

"You mean like her?" He pointed his chin towards the entrance.

I turned and saw a large pair of black ears and a red polka-dot bow poking up from behind a bunch of back-slapping adults.

"Thanks, Mr. Dakin!"

"See you in school, Josh . . . but, hey! No running in the hall!"

I wiggled through the crowd. I found Mouse Lady by the ticket table chatting with Reverend Muncaster, but no Raylene. I was just going to go over and see if they knew where she was when something weird happened. One second Mouse Lady was talking and smiling, the next second her head was on the Reverend's shoulder and her ears had fallen onto the floor and she was crying her eyes out.

Reverend Muncaster patted her back and went, "No, no, no, no, no, Claire. It's not your fault. I'm sure you didn't mean to upset her. You know how hard it can be to talk about. She'll be fine. One of our guys will find her. My guess is she just needs some alone time."

And that's when it dawned on me why Raylene must have wanted to rent a brother.

I felt kind of cold and goosebumpy. My eyes stung around the rims. I didn't feel so mad at her anymore.

Part of me wanted to go look for her and see if she was okay, but, by then, Dad and Sharon were in the lobby and bugging me to leave, so I did.

I had a feeling that's what Raylene would have wanted.

CHAPTER 20

Albertina somehow managed to get my cell phone number. She called the next afternoon. She had another big case she needed help with.

Before I had time to decide whether it was a good idea to get dragged into one of her schemes again, she went, "Meet me outside the Professional Centre in fifteen. I'll be parked in the usual place. The girl's coming too . . . Oh, yeah, and forget about being home for dinner." Then she hung up.

Dad was meeting some guy about being best man at his wedding. I knew he wouldn't be home for dinner either. I threw on some cleanish clothes and made sure I'd gotten the strawberry-blond goo out of my eyebrows.

The girl.

I'd thought about Raylene non-stop since I'd heard what the Mouse Lady said at Bounce Back. I was scared to see her again. I was scared she'd be sad, or angry, or different, or that I wouldn't know what to say.

I hoped I looked okay.

I ran all the way to the Professional Centre. Just like Albertina said, her lime-green subcompact was parked in its usual spot, humping the fire hydrant. I climbed in the front seat. She was busy reattaching her left eyelash, so she pretty much ignored me. Raylene showed up a couple minutes later. It looked like she'd had to run to get there too.

"So what's this one about?" she said, and stretched out in the back seat, panting, smiling, giving me a little punch *hello* in the shoulder. Same as ever. I gave her a little punch back and tried not to smile too hard.

Albertina put that crazy-eyed Joker-in-drag face on again. She slammed the car into gear and pulled into traffic. The whole time, she was looking in her purse for something.

"Here," she said and threw a brochure at me. "Take a gander at this."

It was a flyer advertising the opening of a new restaurant called Lorenzo's at the Chebucto Mall. I took a look and shrugged. It had everything you'd expect: pictures of pretty people eating, a message from the owner, lots of stuff about free-range, local, Grade A, whatever.

"So?" I said.

"So?!" Dangerous lane change. Lots of honking and raised fingers. "This is the big one, kiddies!"

"I thought Janie was the big one." Raylene was leaning in between the two front seats.

"Different kind of big. This is the man who started my whole career. I thought he'd never show his face around here again. Must have figured I'd be dead by now. Ha! I'll show him dead!"

"Who is he?" I asked.

She tapped the picture of a guy on the back of the flyer, and I read the name. "Lorenzo Martinelli?"

That got a bark. "Close. Wade Schmidt. He's packed on the blubber but I'd recognize him anywhere. I see him every day of my life. That's the face I aim at when I blow my nose. That's the body I shove into the trash bag on garbage day. That's the head I crush when—"

"He rip off a bunch of old people or something?" Raylene cut her off before we got any more grisly details.

"They weren't old when he started, but they sure as hell were by the time he was done with them. The lives that guy ruined. Made off with a ton of money. And now he has the nerve to come back here with his *fine dining experience*. I'm going fricassee his ass."

The mall was packed that day, so Albertina had to park miles from the restaurant. She got out of the car, then made me help her into the wheelchair. That might just have been part of her act, but who knows? She looked tired, although she sure sounded like her old self.

"Saw the flyer yesterday and immediately called up an old buddy of mine. Don's been trying to get Schmidt almost as long as I have. His ears sure perked up when he heard that snake was at it again. Said there'd been rumours Schmidt was up to some funny business. Said he'd dig around for new dirt and get back to me ASAP."

She took a big breath and smiled. "You know, whenever I feel like I'm getting soft, I do some work on the Schmidt-head inquiry and—hoo, boy!—I'm spitting mad again in no time. Ahhh, nothing like a little undiluted evil to get the blood flowing. Better than any of those useless pills Randy keeps fobbing off on me, that's for damn sure."

Lorenzo's had a corner space at the mall with fancy wooden doors facing the parking lot. A big banner said, "Try our opening week specials!" We checked the menu and went in, even though the prices were definitely out of my range. (If Albertina's nano-apartment and the fact that Raylene didn't even have a cell phone were anything to go by, I'd say they were out of theirs too.)

"Don't worry," Albertina said when I mentioned it. "We're not going to be paying for the meal." That didn't make me feel any better. Dine 'n' dash with Albertina. Not even in my worst nightmares had I considered that possibility.

We got a table and Albertina made us order the three most expensive things on the menu.

While we were waiting, she pushed the flyer at me. "Hold your nose and read this. I can only presume *advertorial* is Italian for BS."

I started reading out loud. Raylene peered at the flyer over my shoulder. It was like she was giving off pure carbon monoxide or something. I could hear my brain cells clunking on the floor, little black x's for eyes, birds chirping around their heads, goofy lovestruck smiles on their faces. I had to concentrate just to get the words out.

"'Success in the corporate world, of course, is gratifying,' says the renowned restaurateur and philanthropist, 'but it's nothing compared to giving back to the community. Over the years, I've—'"

"Stop. Stop. Thought I could handle it, but I can't. One more word, and so help me, I'll flip my cookies." Albertina didn't look like she was joking. She was pale and splotchy and damp around the forehead. I figured too much excitement for one day. The other old people I knew always had a nap after activity hour.

She started doing that panting thing she'd done in the pharmacy, but this time, it wasn't for her pills.

"That's him. That's him!" She jabbed her head towards the back of the restaurant.

I was getting a bit of that buzz myself. A little nervous. A little excited. Raylene was biting her lip and laughing. My guess is she was feeling that way too.

I turned around as if I were checking out the decor. A guy in a dark suit was shaking hands with a bunch of other guys in dark suits. "Which one?"

"Bowling ball on chicken legs."

I looked again. Suraj couldn't have said it better.

"Cam, pass your phone." Albertina snapped her fingers at me. "Your phone! I got to get this."

I handed it to her, but by the time she figured out that you have to a) touch the video icon to b) start recording, Lorenzo had disappeared and the waiter was at the table with our meals.

Raylene had the lobster, Albertina had the scampi (which is apparently just a fancy name for shrimp), and I had the capon (which is apparently just a fancy name for chicken).

"You mean, *castrated* chicken," Raylene said, then shrugged. "Random fact." We both laughed.

"Do these smell funny to you?" Albertina said in a loud voice. The people at the next table turned and looked. She held out her plate to them and scrunched up her nose. "Get a whiff of that, would ya? I mean, woohoo! Something's funky. What about you? How you liking the food? It's a little . . ." She wobbled her hand back and forth. "Don't you think?"

They made some embarrassed mumbles, then went back to picking at their meals. Albertina tried the same shtick with the people on the other side. They were polite enough, but asked the waiter to move them to another table next time he wandered by. He was a long, skinny guy with a nose to match. The crow-eye he gave us when he had to reset their table totally cracked Raylene up.

I couldn't figure out what Albertina was complaining about. I actually found the food pretty good. But then again, anything I don't have to scrape mould off feels like fine dining to me.

Albertina barely touched her scampi.

"Want some of mine?" I said. I still had a whole leg left.

She went, "Ugh. *Pfft*," which I took to mean *no*. She wiped her forehead with her napkin. Half her face came off with it.

"Y'okay?" Raylene reached out to touch her hand but she batted it away.

"Too much yackety-yack from you guys, not to mention that stinking shrimp." She straightened her wig. "Think I may need my pills. Why don't you two go get them for me? They're in the car."

"I'll stay here with you," Raylene said.

"No, git! I mean it." She pulled her giant key chain out of her purse and shook it in my face until I took it. "It'll take both you numbskulls to find the car and make

120

it back here alive. Now, out of my way. I'm going to figure out how this thing works if it kills me."

We left her pushing random icons on my phone and
swearing. "And do me a favour. Don't hurry back. I need
some jeezly me-time."

When we got outside, Raylene turned to me and
said, "You know the one thing I hate more than a creep?"

I'd almost forgotten how irritating she could be.

"A creep who can't run."

She took off across the parking lot. I took off too.
Even in the boots, she was pretty fast, but I still got there
first.

CHAPTER 21

We looked everywhere in the car, but the only interesting discovery we made was that Albertina had a nasty animal-cracker habit. Under all the other junk, the floor was littered with three-legged rhinos and decapitated monkeys. There were bunches of files too, a few more pictures of Eldon, and what I thought was a venomous tropical insect but turned out to be a spare set of false eyelashes. (I don't care what Raylene said. She'd have screamed too if she'd found it clamped onto *her* groin.)

After about ten minutes, we gave up on the search and started walking back to the restaurant. "I bet the pills are in that massive purse of hers," I said. "That thing scares me. Wouldn't be surprised to find body parts in there too."

"Got to put 'em somewhere," Raylene said. "And she might have a few more by the time we get back. I bet this was just some scam she dreamed up to get us out of there. She was probably planning a kamikaze attack on poor old Lorenzo and didn't want us to get splattered. I mean, you know how considerate she is and everything."

That made me laugh. I could totally picture Albertina going after that little dough ball. She'd eradicate him. Raylene and I spent the rest of the walk across the parking lot pondering some of the moves she might use on him. (The naked-flaming-body-slam was my personal favourite.)

I couldn't remember the last time I was so happy. I managed to talk Raylene into playing with a puppy we found sticking his nose out a car window for a while. I told her it was to give Albertina her "jeezly me-time," but really what I was doing was getting some Raylene-time for myself.

When we got back to the restaurant twenty minutes later, people were pouring out the door. Security guards in black uniforms and modified mullets were directing everyone away from the building and onto the sidewalks. Something was happening. It was sort of exciting.

"You *were* kidding about the kamikaze thing, weren't you?" I said.

"That's not funny." Raylene crossed her hands on her collarbone and looked at me with big eyes.

We pushed our way over to one of the guards. "What's going on?" I said. "Why's everyone leaving?"

"There's been a medical emergency. You're going to have to move back."

"Can we go in? Our"—I didn't even have to think about it—"grandmother's in there."

"Sorry. You'll have to move back. She'll be coming out like everyone else. Please. Step. Back."

People were standing around with their hands over their mouths. One lady was leaning against her friend, sobbing. Parents with fake smiles on their faces were rushing little kids back to cars. An ambulance pulled up and the crowd split to let it pass. Guys ran in with a stretcher.

A couple minutes later, they came back out. They weren't moving so fast any more. A blanket was draped over the stretcher. All you could see of the body was a little tuft of tangerine hair sticking out the top.

CHAPTER 22

When I was twelve, Dad went out with this lady named Kim. Kim Egerton. She was really nice. The type of person who would have fallen in love with him even if he hadn't lost the weight or had all the dental work done. She taught little kids with learning disabilities so she was kind of perfect for us. Fun, but no pushover. Her snacks were excellent and she always made sure we had everything back in its proper place before we watched TV.

I was crazy about her, and so was Dad.

I was pretty sure she was going to move in with us. She was around all the time. Then this one night, I woke up. Maybe I heard noises or maybe I was thirsty. I don't remember but it was late, I know that. I stumbled into the living room. Dad and Kim jumped up off the futon all red-faced and embarrassed. I thought I'd caught them at it or something.

Dad went, "What are you doing up at this hour?" The squeak in his voice was just so hilarious I started going, "Dad and Kimmy, up a tree, K-I-S-S-I-N-G. First comes love . . ."

Things went kind of nuts after that.

Dad lunged at me as if I'd said the F-word at a baptism or something. Then Kim was bolting the other way, her hands over her face and her legs kind of clumsy and flailing, and the door was opening and slamming shut and Dad was hustling me into my room, and then she was gone. It probably took all of ten seconds.

I was back in bed with the lights out and the blankets up around my ears before I could decipher what my sleepy little lizard brain had picked up right away. The look on Dad's face. The look on hers. The tears.

Kim was gone. Like, for good. I never found out exactly what had happened, but it was clearly over. I could hear Dad swearing quietly in the living room.

It was the same this time. I saw the orange hair and I just knew. I probably even knew before that. I bet I knew as soon as I saw the security guards. My mind might not have, but the skin on the back of my neck sure did.

I just sort of stood there in the crowd like I was a specimen in a glass jar with everything swirling round me at half-speed. The paramedics, the people from the restaurant, the random gawkers who suddenly swarmed the parking lot as if someone had just kicked an anthill. Nothing was quite real.

Albertina is gone.

It had taken me weeks to believe that Kim had left. I'd kept hoping sitcom rules would apply and everything would be okay. Just before the final commercial on our little DIY episode of *One and A Half Men*, she'd walk back in the door and there would be hugs and kisses and delicious snacks at a clean kitchen table again. It didn't happen that way, of course.

I understood that right away with Albertina but of course Albertina was no Kim. I mean, I barely knew her. And I'm older now too. I get it. Things don't always work out the way they're supposed to. You just make the best of it until the worst happens, and then you do it all over again. But still. Albertina was dead, but somewhere Kim was alive and getting on with her life. This time it was forever.

I watched the paramedics heave themselves into the ambulance and drive away. After a while, things sped up to normal, and cars honked and sounds came out again when people moved their mouths to say something.

"That was her," I finally said.

Raylene nodded. Her arms were on either side of me like she was hugging a harp.

"She's dead," I said. "They covered her up."

Raylene turned her face into my chest and nodded again.

I thought of suicide and her brother—and if that's what had happened to him, how much worse this must be for her than me. I tried to say the right thing.

"She was sick. It's a blessing. She's not suffering anymore." I didn't really believe that. It was just Almost Family stuff. Stuff people say at funerals. Stuff I'd memorized.

"It was so fast." Raylene squeegeed the tears off her face with the back of her hand.

"That's good, isn't it?" I said. "You wouldn't want it to have dragged on."

"I didn't get a chance to say goodbye. I never get to say goodbye."

Raylene shook her head and did some weird thing with her mouth, then kind of burrowed back into my chest. Maybe she'd been right and I was a creep, but I sort of stopped thinking about Albertina or dead brothers and just concentrated on Raylene's arms and face and that bare strip of her stomach against my side.

We were still standing like that when the security guard showed up.

"This is them, Officer," he said. He'd brought a cop with him.

Raylene jumped away from me.

CHAPTER 23

Raylene stopped crying. The cop was nice. We explained Albertina was our grandmother, or at least sort of our grandmother but not really, and he just nodded like *yeah, okay*. Those guys have seen everything.

He said, "You want to sit?" We said, "No," then he said, "Sure? You had an awful shock." But we said, "It's all right" so he asked us her name and where she lived, then he said we should call our parents. I told him Albertina had my phone so he went and found it in the restaurant for me.

When he came back, he said, "Just a couple minutes, guys. I need a little more information from you." He took out his notebook. "Your names?"

"Cam, or I guess I should say, Cameron P—"

"Oops, hold on." The radio on the cop's shoulder was buzzing. He raised his finger and spoke into it, then he said, "Sorry. Hate to do this. I'll be right back," and walked over to the ambulance. A paramedic was holding an oxygen mask over a lady's face with one hand and waving to the cop with the other.

I wanted to see what was up but Raylene grabbed my hand and ran. Ran even faster than before. I went, "What? What? What are you doing? The cop. He's. We have to. We're supposed to. Stop!"

And she went, "Shut up. Move it—I said, move it!" It was as if Albertina's spirit had left her body and immediately taken over Raylene's. The girl who'd been sniffling into my chest disappeared.

I was—I'm not kidding—terrified. I might think I like undercover work, but the fact is I come from a long yellow line of wusses. I do not, under any circumstances, abscond from the police. I was so scared I couldn't even appreciate the soft, pound-cakey fact that Raylene was holding my hand.

She dragged me back to the car. She beeped the doors open and went, "Get in, get in, get in." Then she rammed in the key and cranked up the ignition. "You know how to drive?!" I said.

"I know how to drive a tractor." She lurched out of the parking space.

"That's not the same thing. That is *not* the same thing."

"You see a tractor anywhere?"

"No."

"So we're taking the car."

"This is *not* taking. This is stealing."

"Maybe. But we can't just leave it here."

"Yes, we can. We *absolutely* can."

"No, we can't." She gave a red Audi a light sanding on the way past. "That cop would find it and I don't like that cop."

"What are you talking about? He was nice!"

She was holding the steering wheel way up on the top. Her knuckles were white. "You clearly don't know cops."

"I do so. Ryan Sumner is a cop and he hired me as his nephew to . . . Watch where you're going!" We hit the curb and bounced back into the exit lane.

"You don't know cops. I know cops. I don't want to talk to them. And I'm sure as hell Albertina wouldn't want us talking to them either. And she wouldn't want them rooting through her car."

"Please. Watch. The road."

"She probably has important stuff in here."

"What? Animal crackers and pictures of Eldon?! We just went through every inch of the car. That's all there is. And old Kleenexes."

"And files. What about the files? She was working on some cases. The big ones—Janie? Lorenzo? Remember? What do you think we were doing here? There might be information in there we'll need."

"*We'll* need? What do you mean *we'll* need?"

My concerns were apparently unimportant. She turned on to the highway and veered way into the outside lane. People honked at her. She waved as if they were old buddies and got back on track.

I had my arms braced against the dashboard and my teeth clamped over my lower lip.

"Would you stop that? I couldn't possibly be a worse driver than Albertina, and you survived her. So quit it, would you? I'll get the car to her place, then we'll figure out what to do next. Okay?"

"Okay." Like I had a choice.

"You know the way?"

"Yeah."

"Then you're going to have to open your eyes and show me."

CHAPTER 24

She stomped on the brakes like she was killing taran-
tulas, and I could feel my brain slam into my eardrum
every time she attempted a left turn, but she got us there
in one piece.

"See?" she said. "Not so bad. Just put your head
between your knees for a minute, then we'll go inside
and get her stuff."

"Why are we getting her stuff?" I watched the drool
sway over my sneaker. "What stuff?"

"We'll know it when we see it." That was Albertina
speaking through Raylene again. I didn't like where this
was going.

It took her a while to figure out which one of
Albertina's gazillion keys opened which door, but we
made it up to her apartment without anybody seeing
us. Raylene whispered, "Look for anything, I mean anything, about Lorenzo Martinelli, Wade Martinelli, Wade
Schmidt, or Janie Atkinson."

"Aikens."

"Janie Anyone. You see the name Janie/Jane/June/Jezebel—whatever—you grab the file."

"Then what do we do?"

"We take everything we can find and put it all in the car."

"No. No. That's. That's, like, disturbing a crime scene or something. That's a—"

"Albertina died at the restaurant. This isn't a crime scene."

"It will be once we steal files from it."

She laughed like I'd made a joke and kept rummaging through the papers. She looked under the bed, behind the chair, in the closet. Papers were flying around as if some mini tornado had just touched down smack dab in the middle of apartment 312.

I could hear the person next door turn on the TV. I recognized the *Entertainment Tonight* theme music. Someone was going to catch us here and then we'd go to jail, and Dad would have to visit me *and* Dalton. He wasn't going to be very happy about that.

"Raylene," I whispered. She stopped and put her hands on her hips but it wasn't to listen to me. She was staring at the wall, chewing on the inside of her cheeks, thinking.

"Rayleeeeeeeene."

"We're never going to be able to look through all this," she mumbled and I thought *phew, finally.*

"We've got to be reasonable." And I thought *yes!*

"Let's just grab all the files around her bed." And I thought *nooo!* "That's probably where she did most of her reading. The old files are probably stacked over there, don't you think?"

I thought we should get out of there. That's what I thought.

Raylene disappeared into the kitchen and came back with a bunch of plastic grocery bags. "C'mon. Get moving," she whispered. "I want to be long gone by the time the cops get here."

I did too.

I really did.

I got moving.

CHAPTER 25

There's a twenty-four-hour supermarket not far from our place.

"No one will find it here," Raylene said, and parked the car at the far end of the lot. By "parked the car" I mean "slammed into the curb at top speed and lurched to a stop."

She leaned into the back seat and pulled out a bunch of files, dumped half on my lap, and kept the rest for herself. "Okay. Let's go through everything and see what we can find."

"No," I said.

She put her elbow on the steering wheel and looked at me.

"No," I said. "Tomorrow, maybe, but not now. I feel sick."

"Put your head between—"

"That's not going to help."

"Yes, it is."

"How's that going to help? Albertina just died. We ran away from the police, stole a car, committed a burglary. You wanna know why I feel sick? That's why I feel sick. It doesn't help, of course, that you drive like a—"

"Like a what?" All cute and jokey.

"I don't know."

"Seriously. Like a what?"

"Nothing." She was annoying me.

"C'mon. You can't just start to say something like that, then leave it."

I shook my head. It hurt. "I said I don't know."

"You do so. C'mon . . ." She had this goofy smile on her face. She wasn't going to stop.

"Okay. Like a gecko."

"I drive like a gecko?" She laughed.

"See! That's what I mean! My brain's fried. You fried my brain."

"Seriously—*a gecko*?"

"It was the only thing I could think of that was fast and jerky and had absolutely no understanding of the rules of the road."

"Okay. Gecko's fair."

"Quit laughing. This isn't funny. I can't do this. We've got to call someone, figure out what we should be doing."

Somebody needed to claim the body or something,

didn't they? We couldn't just run away and pretend nothing had happened.

Raylene paused. "Like who?" At least she sounded halfway serious now.

It was a good question. Dad? He'd freak. Suraj? Lot of good that would do. His parents? OMG. Raylene's parents? Who knew if she even had them? I thought of some of the people who worked for Almost Family. Frank— incapacitated. Doreen—usually inebriated. Barbara— borderline insane. Kev, Vernon, Jenn—I ruled them all out too. There were reasons these so-called grown-ups could only get work renting themselves out occasionally as relatives. I realized, weirdly, that Albertina was probably the only person I could have called. She was the only person who conceivably would have had experience with something like this and she was gone.

I suggested the next best thing. "Reverend Muncaster. At St. Cuthbert's. That's where I met Albertina."

Raylene didn't say no, not that it would have mattered what she said. I couldn't handle this anymore. I got out my phone.

"I just heard," Reverend Muncaster said when I told her Albertina had died. "It's all over social media."

"It is? What's everyone saying?"

"The police aren't identifying her but bystanders described the victim on Facebook, and I guessed.

Albertina has been a regular at St. Cuthbert's for quite a while. There aren't many people you'd confuse her with."

No kidding.

"Twitter's reporting she was poisoned by some bad shrimp at that new restaurant in the mall. That true?"

I said I didn't know. I gave her a cleaned-up version of my story with Albertina: doing the grandson thing, helping her with her business, whatever. I kept it vague. I left out Raylene and all the stuff about the various felonies we'd committed. I told her Dad didn't know about it. She didn't ask why. Reverend Muncaster's relatively cool, as religious fanatics go.

"So what should we do now?" I asked. "Shouldn't her next of kin be notified or something?"

"To the best of my knowledge, it was just Albertina. She told me once she'd had a family but—well, I'm not sure what happened there. All I know is it was source of great sadness for her. Anyway, my dear, you leave it to me. I'll get in touch with the police, get the obit in the paper. All you have to do is make it to the church by three on Tuesday."

I felt so much better.

"It's a very sad day," Reverend Muncaster said, then she hung up. It sounded like she was going to cry.

We sat in the car without saying anything for a long

time, then Raylene, kind of joking, went, "I don't think Albertina would appreciate a moment of silence. She's not that type."

"Wasn't."

"What?"

"*Wasn't* that type," I said. "Albertina's dead."

Raylene tucked her lips into her mouth, and her eyes got all shiny, and she turned away. I didn't mean to upset her.

She eventually said, "I'm hungry," and I tried to get us back into that jokey thing by picking a monkey part off the floor and going, "Can I offer you an animal cracker?"

She turned to me, looking more or less okay again. "Not *that* hungry. Let's get something at the super-market. I've got money."

We locked the car and headed in. It was one of those giant grocery stores that sells everything from buffalo burgers to all-terrain vehicles. At the far end, there was a huge food court with a bunch of franchises.

"I suddenly feel the need for pizza," I said.

"Here." She handed me six bucks, enough for the combo deal. I was too hungry to worry where the cash was coming from.

"I'm going for Thai. Meet you back at the car in, say, ten minutes?"

I nodded. She left for the other side of the food court.

I got in the lineup. Raylene was already gone by the time my double-pepperoni, bacon, and pineapple came up, and she wasn't at the car when I got there either.

It took me twenty minutes to realize she'd taken off again.

CHAPTER 26

I woke up at three the next morning. My mouth was dry from the pizza—or maybe just from having the life sucked out of me.

I felt bad about the whole Raylene thing.

No. I felt mad.

So something terrible had happened in her life. Big deal. I didn't care. Reverend Muncaster was wrong about me. I wasn't a saint. Bad things happen to lots of people. Doesn't give them the right to treat other people like garbage. Doesn't give them the right to just ditch a person, over and over again.

I stared at the just-barely-fluorescent stars some kid before me had stuck on the bedroom ceiling. The stars made me think of heaven, which made me think of Albertina, which, frankly, was kind of funny. I doubted she was anywhere near the place.

A tear popped into my eye and sizzled like acid.

Where the hell did that come from?

I hardly knew Albertina. She was funny and every-thing and she did totally nail Dr. Blaine and save all those old people a bunch of money. But she was also loud and pushy and she tricked me and insulted me and said mean things about my dad and our business. All in all, not someone I'd generally cry over.

I figured it was just the shock of having her die that was getting to me, but then I thought *no*. I'd actually known quite a few people who'd died. Even seen them die. Dad always makes us stay with our clients right to the end. He gets attached to the old guys, even the mean, bitter, delusional ones. We're all just human, he says. No one's perfect. We all need love.

He wouldn't desert them in their hour of need.

Which made me think of Raylene deserting me again and I felt better for a little while. I was definitely the good guy in this situation.

Which made me think what a jerk I was. Getting ditched at the supermarket is hardly being deserted on your deathbed-slash-table-for-three.

And that's when I figured out where that tear came from.

I switched on the light. Albertina had died alone. I pictured her at Lorenzo's, going grey, grabbing her throat, maybe squawking a bit while people at the other tables all pretended they didn't notice until, of course, her lifeless body clunked on the floor, at which point, they *had* to do something, i.e., cry piteously for the benefit of everyone videotaping her last minutes on their cell phones.

Sad way to go. For anyone. Even Albertina.

Who I realized I liked way more than I was letting on.

I decided I was going to make it up to her. I switched off the light. I slept okay after that.

CHAPTER 27

Luckily, that Tuesday just happened to be when Dad was taking one of his mothers to lunch and a lecture on feline ancestry at the Museum of Natural History. I had the whole day to get ready.

I was worried there wouldn't be many mourners so I checked my bank account. $122.28.

If the funeral didn't run long, that would be enough for Frank and Doreen and one more Almost Family employee. Maybe Lindsay.

No, not Lindsay. She still had that thing for Dad and it was getting embarrassing.

I called Kev because he had a car and could get them all there and also because he knew about giving Frank toffee if he started making inappropriate remarks. (It sticks to his dentures, so it can be used to distract him.) I also asked Kev to make sure the others didn't blab to Dad about this little gig. (Kev was in a biker gang for ages so he understands the whole code-of-silence thing.)

Then I made Suraj call in sick at the deli. I rooted around until I found an old suit from junior high that more or less fit him. We stapled up the legs and blacked out an unpleasant stain on the lapel and he looked okay. I even convinced him to do something with the scuzzy bacterial culture he insisted on referring to as his "beard."

That made five of us. Not even enough to fill a pew but at least the church wouldn't be totally empty. (It can happen. Trust me.)

Suraj and I took the bus to St. Cuthbert's. I was relieved when we got there and saw quite a few cars in the parking lot. Not quite bingo night, but close. Albertina was dead and she was still surprising me.

We headed in. Reverend Muncaster was talking to someone by the bird-bath thing they baptize babies in.

She patted down my collar and straightened my tie and said, "Well. Didn't you do Albertina proud," then told us there were seats reserved for us up front.

"Don't I have to bow or kneel or make elaborate hand gestures or something?" Suraj whispered on the way up the aisle.

I rolled my eyes.

"What?" he said. "How am I supposed to know? Not like I've been to church before."

"You have to whip yourself with a cat-o'-nine-tails

146

while chanting in Latin—but that comes later. I'll tell you when."

"Really? I didn't think they did that anymore." I could tell by the look on his face he was thinking of his series again.

The Almost Family crew was about midway in. Kev saw me and shrugged like *I thought you said nobody was going to be here?* I shrugged back. I nodded at Dr. Ewan and Randy the pharmacist a little farther to the front, then found our places. There was a leaflet on the pew with the title *Celebrating the Life of Albertina Marie Legge* and a picture of her when she was young.

"Whoa. Betty-Flintstone-goes-to-the-rodeo," Suraj whispered. The big inappropriate smile on his face faded when the lady behind us pointedly cleared her throat.

The organ started playing and Reverend Muncaster walked up to the front, and that's when I gave up all hope of Raylene showing. I told myself I was just mad for Albertina's sake, but who was I kidding?

Prayers were said and hymns sung, but I didn't really zone in until the eulogy started.

Reverend Muncaster stood at the pulpit, her arms crossed, her hands hidden in the sleeves of her robe. She smiled at the congregation. (Dad always said she'd perfected the all-purpose sad/sorry/compassionate, but ultimately-hopeful, smile.)

"I have a confession to make," she said. "When Albertina found out she didn't have much time left, she took me aside and gave me strict instructions about her funeral. There were two rules I was absolutely not, under any circumstances, allowed to break.

"I broke the first one earlier today, but Lord knows, not for want of trying. She made me promise I wouldn't get up here looking my usual frumpy self, but I just could not get those darn false eyelashes on."

Big crowd-pleaser. Hearty laughter.

"The second rule I haven't broken yet, but I will. You can probably picture this: Albertina leaning back in her wheelchair and saying, 'All right, Your Grace. None of this nonsense about what a fine human being I was. Just sprinkle me with incense or barbecue sauce or whatever the hell it is you do and put me out with the garbage Wednesday morning.'

"Sorry, Albertina. But I can't do that. I've got to get in my two cents' worth before the garbage truck comes by.

"I knew Albertina for a long time but that doesn't mean I knew her well. She wasn't shy about telling me what she thought of my sermon or my outfit or my choice in men for that matter, but she wasn't too forthcoming otherwise. Over the years, however, I did glean that she'd known enormous sorrow in her life. After Eldon died, she tried to get back on her feet. She straightened herself out. Fought off her demons. She eventually married again, but the only good to come out of that, she told me, were a few hog-calling trophies. After the divorce, more darkness followed. It was only when she gave herself over to helping others that she could truly live again.

"And she did. Her life became about making sure that others never suffered as she had. I see heads nodding. I know that's why so many of you are here today. She was your champion. She fought to make the world a better place for you, or for your family, or even just for some stranger she'd seen mistreated. In Albertina, we saw how one tiny person with nothing more than love and determination and an outlandish sense of style can slay giants.

"So, again, I apologize to Albertina for breaking my promise and 'wasting your jeezly time,' but I ask that in memory of our dear brave friend, you do two things. One: go out and help someone less fortunate than yourself. And two: do something with that awful hair of yours.

"And now, please rise for the singing of 'My Wild Irish Rose.'"

CHAPTER 28

It was the bridesmaid-from-hell dress. Bright pink. Puffed sleeves. Bow in the back. I barely recognized her.

"What? You don't like it?" Raylene had popped out at us from behind a tree at the far end of the parking lot just as we were leaving. She was even wearing lipstick. In fact, if I'm not mistaken, the fuchsia lipstick Albertina kept on her key chain.

She held out her skirt and spun around like a little kid playing princess or a lady in an adult diaper commercial.

"Well, *I* like it." Suraj may be my best friend but he's never been one to miss an opportunity.

I went, "Why weren't you at the funeral?"

She stopped twirling but kept the laugh on her face. "I was. At the back. Got in a bit late. I couldn't find any shoes at the Sally Ann that matched, so I had to go to Frenchie's Bargain Shop."

She pointed her toe. Her shoes were high-heeled

and pointed and covered in useless buckles. Suraj said, "Ooh. Steampunk-Cinderella."

"I know. Fabulous, aren't they?"

"Bit disrespectful to Albertina, coming in late like that, don't you think?" I wasn't going to let her think this was just some joke.

"Please. Disrespectful would be arriving at her funeral in shoes that didn't match."

Couldn't argue with that. Luckily, I didn't even have to try. Someone tapped my shoulder. I turned around.

Dr. Ewan and his big, sad face.

"There you are. Thought I'd missed you."

I introduced him to Suraj, then he gave Raylene and me each a bear hug.

"I was a big fan of your grandmother's," he said. "She was a real old-fashioned broad—and I mean that in the best way possible. I was always sore by the time she left my office, either from laughing or having her tear a strip off me. I'm going to miss her—or at least miss most of her."

We chuckle-nodded at that, then stood around awkwardly, scuffling our feet.

"Listen," he said after a while. "I'm not sure it's my business to say this, but I've been worried about you guys. I understand Albertina died on your watch."

"We weren't actually there," Raylene said. "We went

to get her pills from the car, but by the time we got back, she was, you know, like, um, gone." Her voice cracked. We all pretended not to notice.

"That's what I wanted to talk to you about. Randy Norwood—the pharmacist downstairs from me? I think you know him. We'd been conferring about Albertina for a while. He was worried she was stockpiling meds in case she needed them."

"Needed them for what?" I said.

"Suicide." Raylene sounded so sure.

Dr. Ewan rocked his head side to side. "I prefer end-of-life self-care. Her prognosis wasn't good. She'd told me many times that there was no way she was ending up in hospital like some voodoo doll with a bunch of needles sticking out of her. The day she died, in fact, I'd had a little talk with her. I told her she had a week or so left—if she was lucky. I tried to convince her to go somewhere she'd be comfortable but, well, you saw how she reacted to that. She was determined to do things her own way."

"You think that's what she did?" I was shocked. "Took a bunch of pills while we were gone?"

He curled his bottom lip, shook his head. "No sign of that. And it wasn't the shrimp either. I think she died when she did because she decided *not* to take her pills. I've got a sneaking suspicion she felt her heart acting up and thought, *what the hell? I'm in a nice restaurant. Just had a delicious meal with my beloved grandkids. May as well leave on a high note.* She got you out of the way to make sure you missed the gruesome stuff, then just let nature take its course. It would have been relatively fast. What we in the business call a clutch-and-keel. Felt a pain. Grabbed her throat. A few minutes later, it was all over."

Raylene had taken off her glasses and was wiping the tears away with her palm.

"You shouldn't feel bad about it." Dr. Ewan put his hand on my shoulder. "If it hadn't happened then, it would have happened the next day." There was a long, relatively awkward pause while we pulled ourselves together, then he said, "So. Your older sister make it today?"

Good thing about my Almost Family training is that I'm pretty used to having things thrown at me. I'd already shaken my head in what I hoped was a convincing manner before I realized what he was talking about. Oh, right. That older sister. The one who was supposedly looking after Albertina.

"She was too upset."

"Too bad. I always wanted to meet her. Your grandmother thought the world of her."

We smiled and shook hands and promised to come by if we ever needed anything from him, then Dr. Ewan headed off to his car.

"O. Emmm. G." Raylene had stopped dead. She was gawking at something near the church. "You see what I see?"

Suraj turned to look but I didn't. I was worried if I took my eyes off her even for a second, she'd disappear again, and I didn't want that. As it was, she seemed to be slipping back behind the tree.

"What?" he said.

"That guy talking to Reverend Muncaster. That's him."

"Who?"

"Wade Freaking Schmidt."

"You mean, Mr. Lorenzo?"

"Yup."

"Whoa. Ballsy move." I'd already told Suraj the whole story. "Didn't think he'd be on the guest list."

I couldn't resist anymore. I turned, too. "And that other guy's the waiter," I said.

"You sure?" Raylene was squinting out from behind the tree.

"He's waving at us." I waved back. "I'm sure."

CHAPTER 29

Raylene was in a rage and also the driver's seat. A bad combination.

"No. C'mon! Think about it! Seriously." She glared at me as if this was my fault.

"Eyes on the road!" I screamed. I don't know how she'd talked us into Albertina's car again.

"Relax. Jeez. No one was even *on* the sidewalk. Okay. Listen. Let's say Dr. Ewan is correct and Albertina killed herself."

"He didn't say 'killed herself.'"

"Okay. *Let herself die.* Better?"

"More accurate."

"Fine. Why would she do it at Lorenzo's?"

"She couldn't stand the wallpaper a second longer?" Suraj was trying to add a little levity to the situation. Raylene wasn't amused. He went back to playing with my phone. (I let him look at it just so he didn't fall too far behind, technologically speaking. All he has is an ancient clamshell and he has to share that with his brothers. Tuesday wasn't his day.)

"I don't know," I said. "She'd probably just had enough. Old people get that way. Dr. Ewan said . . ."

"No!" Raylene slammed her hand on the dashboard. "Albertina was not *old people*. Albertina was not the type to have *just had enough*. You're not trying. Think!"

I was scared the next thing she'd be slamming into was the car in front of us, so I started thinking.

"To upset him? To annoy him? I don't know. To get back at him?"

"Yes!" Both hands off the wheel for one brief but terrifying moment.

"You're kidding. You don't actually think Albertina was tough or mean or crazy enough to let herself die just to"—I made air quotes—"*get back at someone.*"

"Why are you surprised? She said she was going to fricassee his ass."

"For what?" Suraj said. "Not that that requires a reason."

"No idea," Raylene answered. "That's why we're going back to her apartment."

I crumpled mentally. I'd been under the delusion we were going to get something to eat. I didn't want to go the apartment again. Call me crazy but break-and-enter has never been my thing. Neither is getting arrested, and I just knew we were going to get arrested one of these days.

Raylene turned into the parking lot at Albertina's building. For a second, it looked like she'd decided to play chicken with a large green dumpster, but she swerved just in the nick of time.

"All right, guys. Let's go," she said.

I swallowed, summoned my courage. This had to stop now.

"No," Suraj said before I could open my mouth.

We both turned and stared at him.

"I think you're going to want to see this video first." He handed my phone up to the front seat.

CHAPTER 30

JERKY IMAGES OF THE SALT SHAKER, THEN THE
OVERHEAD LIGHT, THEN BACK TO THE SALT SHAKER,
THEN SUDDENLY ALBERTINA'S BLOODSHOT EYE
APPEARS, ALMOST FILLING THE SCREEN.

Albertina (in an angry whisper): Cam? Cam? Can you
hear me? I have no idea if this jeezly thing is working.

PHONE IS PICKED UP AND SHAKEN, THEN PROPPED UP
AGAIN. IN THE BACKGROUND, A WAITER SCOOTS BY
THE TABLE WITH FOUR DISHES SPREAD OUT ALONG
HIS ARMS.

Albertina (in apparent pain): Okay. Whatever.
Listen, kiddies. (Big breath.) Wish I could hang around
until we nail this bonehead (gravelly laugh) but that
ain't happening. I gotta go with my gut. Any luck (more
coughing) and this'll at least shut the sucker down.

SOUNDS OF ALBERTINA WHEEZING. PHONE SLIDES DOWN ONTO ITS SIDE, THEN IS READJUSTED. WOMAN AT THE TABLE ACROSS THE AISLE TRIES TO LOOK ELEGANT WHILE SLURPING SPAGHETTI.

ALBERTINA'S FACE APPEARS IN THE SCREEN, SIDEWAYS, LIKE A CURIOUS PARROT.

Albertina (slow and croaky): One last thing. Cam. You're a good boy. Look after yourself. Look after Hannah too. (Long pause) Oh, and call that damn agent of your dad's. He needs his own show. (Low groan.) Okay. So long, suckers. It's been a blast.

ALBERTINA'S HAND SWIPES HER PLATE OFF THE TABLE. LOUD CRASH.

Albertina: Help! (Gasp) Help! I've been poisoned! Help! It's the shrimp! Help!

WOMAN AT THE NEXT TABLE DROPS HER FORK AND STANDS UP. SHE BEGINS TO SCREAM. ALBERTINA'S FOOT SWINGS IN AND OUT OF FRAME. PEOPLE CROWD AROUND. THE WAITER PUSHES THROUGH.

Waiter: You okay, lady? Don't worry. I'm getting help. I'm calling 911.

Albertina (feebly): I don't want 911. I want Wade.

Waiter: Wade?

Albertina: The owner, you moron!

Waiter (waving): Signor Martinelli! Signor Martinelli!

WADE HOVES INTO VIEW. HIS FACE IS PINK AND PANICKED. HE LEANS TOWARDS ALBERTINA.

Albertina (attempting to scream to other diners): Don't touch the shrimp! The shrimp will kill you!

Wade: Try to stay calm, ma'am. Everything is going to be okay.

Albertina (tough-girl voice): Yeah. You bet it is, Wade.

Wade: Do I know you?

Albertina (gasping): You did. You knew me well enough to steal every cent I had.

Wade (whispering): I have no idea what you're talking about.

Albertina: Ha! (prolonged coughing) Don't play innocent with me. 1978? Bulwark Investments? My grandchildren know all about it. They're on to you.

Wade (through clenched teeth): I was cleared of all charges in a court of law. That's over and done with.

Albertina: Yeah, well, doesn't mean we're not going to get you. Remember what happened to Al Capone? You're our Al Capone.

Wade (to the crowd): Stand back! Let her get some air.

Wade (whispering to waiter): But not too much.

Albertina (gasping): This is it, Wade. I'm done for. And so are you—once the world find outs what you've been up to. And it will.

ALBERTINA STRUGGLES TO WINK.

Albertina (with one last big effort): It was the shrimp!

A LOUD *CLUNK*. GENERALIZED SCREAMING. SCREEN BLANKED OUT AS PEOPLE CROWD AROUND.

CHAPTER 31

Raylene didn't need to give us another pep talk. Nothing like a little message from the grave to get you moving. We left the car behind the dumpster and snuck up to Albertina's apartment.

As soon as we were inside, Raylene whispered, "Undo me." She turned her back and waved a hand over her shoulder until I realized she meant her dress. Suraj mouthed, *Oh my God. Should I go?* I mouthed back, *Don't. Leave. Me.* Then I pulled down her zipper, my face turned away as if I was worried something would explode when it hit bottom.

Raylene stepped out of the dress. She was wearing her tank top and shorts underneath. Suraj and I regained the use of our legs.

"That's better," she whispered. "Now, let's get at it."

She started wading through files on the floor. "I went through all the stuff we took the other night. Nothing more about Schmidt so it must be in here somewhere. Albertina said she kept everything."

Raylene gave us our instructions via hand signals, then we started tiptoeing around the apartment like a bunch of mimes re-enacting an episode of *CSI*.

She looked in the kitchen. I stuck to the living room. Suraj opened the closet door and files barfed out onto the floor.

Raylene and I both went, "Shush!" like a couple of giant vacuum cleaners. If that didn't alert the neighbours to the presence of intruders, nothing would. We played statues until we were sure no one was coming to arrest us, then got back to work.

We scrabbled around for a good hour. We found broken earrings, tubes of lipstick, cases of eye shadow, hundreds of files, and a crazy number of orthopedic insoles, but not a single thing about Schmidt.

I stood up to stretch and noticed the black cabinet Albertina claimed she kept her makeup in.

Makeup?

I stared at it.

I didn't care what she'd told us. No way something that size was just for makeup.

I tried to open the door but it was locked.

"Raylene," I whispered. "The keys." She handed me Albertina's giant keychain.

I got the right one on the sixth try and the door swung open.

The rest of the apartment looked like a recycling

plant. The inside of the black cabinet looked like an OCD fantasy. No makeup, no junk, no animal crackers, just ten to fifteen files, neatly stacked. It wasn't hard to find Schmidt's. It was on the top and almost as overstuffed as he was.

"Ta-da!" I whispered and waved it over my head.

Suraj did a slo-mo victory dance and a silent one-handed high-five.

Raylene put her hand over her mouth, then her other around my waist, and at that moment, I honestly could not have cared less about Wade Jeezly Schmidt.

"C'mon, c'mon. Put it here." She swept a spot clean on the bed and I opened the file.

There was a picture of a young, skinny Wade from about forty years ago, paper-clipped to the folder. Ski-goggle glasses, nasty plaid jacket, moustache the size of small marsupial.

"Whoa," Suraj went. "Super-Mario-goes-disco-dancing."

"No kidding." I was surprised Albertina had even been able to recognize him.

Raylene flipped up the photo and ran her finger over the information sheet below. "Wade Upton Schmidt. Born: April 12, 1948. Graduated from John Thompson Elementary School, Spryfield Junior High, blah-blah-blah, married So-and-So, divorced. Founder of financial firm Bulwark Investments. Sold shares . . ."

She stopped. Her neck went rigid and her eyes went still, and it was hard not to think of a very cute predator on a nature documentary. She put her finger to her lips and mouthed, *Someone's coming.*

Scuffling of feet. Muffled voices. Key in the lock.

Suraj dove behind the black so-called makeup kit. Raylene jumped into the closet. I stood in the centre of the room, my head tick-tocking back and forth as I looked for a place to hide. Raylene grabbed my hand, pulled me into the closet, and shut us in.

The door to the apartment opened. Someone said, "Here you go. No disrespect. I liked your mother and everything but she sure wasn't much of a housekeeper. You're going to have a devil of a time finding whatever it is you're looking for."

A different voice. "Oh, yeah. Ha-ha. I'm used to the mess. I just need a couple of documents to get the estate settled. I'll find them."

"I'll leave you to it, then. I gotta check on a leak in 407. Back in a few minutes."

The door closed. Whoever was left behind waited a few seconds before he swore, sighed, then started walking around the room.

It was a very small closet we were in. Raylene and I had to stand belly-to-belly just to fit. I could feel her boobs rise every time she breathed and her heart pound when the guy walked over to our side of the room and her whole body shake when it looked like he was going to open the closet door.

Then I heard his knees click and figured he was just looking at the files on the floor in front of the closet. Paper rustling, more swearing, more creaking bones. He seemed to move away.

I could feel Raylene relax. She didn't actually change positions. She just, I don't know, sort of changed states, like in chemistry or something. She went from solid to almost liquid. Sort of melted a bit. I felt the way the crispy biscuit in the middle of the Twix bar must feel when the delicious, chocolatey coating envelops it.

Then Raylene hooked her baby finger around mine.

I considered the possibility that this was a mistake. Maybe she had a weird twitch that I'd never noticed before. But then her next finger hooked around mine too.

And then it was like dominoes or a waterfall or maybe spiders mating or something because all our fingers started entwining until that hand was done and then the other side too and then we just stood like that with our hearts bouncing off each other like hundreds of deranged ping-pong balls.

Sometime thereafter, the door slammed closed and the guy must have left.

CHAPTER 32

"Whaddya mean you didn't hear that? How could you not hear that?" Suraj stuck his fingers through the louvres on the closet door and wiggled them at us. "This is hardly what you'd call a soundproof booth."

Raylene and I were standing in the living room, conspicuously ignoring each other.

Suraj looked back and forth between the two of us, then his eyebrows dropped and his lips went flat. He let us squirm a moment before going, "Tell me you're not serious. We've broken into a dead person's apartment. We could be caught and dragged off in shackles at any moment and you're . . ."

"Shackles?" Raylene whispered. "You're exaggerating."

"No, I'm not."

"Fine. If it's so bad, maybe you should just tell us what we missed so we won't let it happen again." Raylene was unshakeable. Another thing I liked about her.

Suraj ran his hand over his face and shook his head. "You know who it was, don't you?"

Raylene went, "Wade?"

Suraj motioned *close*.

I went, "The waiter?"

He nodded.

"How do you know?"

"Unlike some people, I was paying attention. And I peeked while he was on his phone."

"He was on his phone?" we both whisper-gasped.

"Now you're grossing me out. Yes, he was on his phone. He called someone when he found Schmidt's file."

"He found Schmidt's file?" My voice was back up in the pre-puberty range.

"Found it and took it. And that's not all. He knows you've been here, Raylene."

"Me? How does he know that?"

Suraj flicked her dress up off the floor with his foot.

Raylene scrunched up her face like *that's ridiculous*. "How do you know he saw it? And even if he did, who's to say he knew it was mine?"

"Oh, I know he saw it because, one, how could you not see it? What do you call this colour anyway? My eyes hurt just looking at it. And, two, had you been listening, you would have heard him say—I quote—'The girl's been here.' Dot. Dot. Dot. 'Yes. That girl. From the church parking lot. She left her dress.' And then—this was my favourite part—'I know. We'll have to do something about that.' No bloodthirsty laughter, but it was clearly implied."

"Then what happened?" Raylene had gravitated towards me. We weren't quite touching but close.

"The other guy opened the door—the super or who-ever—and the waiter hung up. He grabbed the file, they made small talk, then they left. I waited a few minutes for my bowels to firm up, then I came over to check how you were doing in the honeymoon suite. I was relieved to see you were no worse for wear."

"Yet," I said.

"Oh, get a room." Suraj air-gagged.

"That's not what I meant."

Raylene went, "Then what did you mean?"

"You saw the video. Albertina seriously *hated* this guy. Makes me think he did something really bad. Maybe would do it again."

Suraj went pale, at least by his standards. "We should call the police."

I said, "No. No police," because after the fit she took in the Lorenzo's parking lot, I knew Raylene wouldn't want police (and, also, because that's what five minutes in a closet with her does to a person's brain).

Suraj looked at me like I was nuts. This was clearly not the world-class chicken he'd come to know and love.

I said, "You want to go to jail? Think about it. How do we explain how we know all this stuff? We're the ones trespassing. We're the ones who stole her car."

"Hey! I didn't steal any car."

"Oh, please, Suraj. You've seen *Law & Order*. Aiding and abetting. Accessory to the fact. Theft over five thousand . . ."

"That car's not worth five thousand!"

"Doesn't matter. Your fingerprints are all over it. And anyway, if Albertina thought the police could deal with this, don't you think she'd have called them herself?"

The answer was no, but Suraj didn't need to know that. The motion was defeated.

Raylene whispered, "We've got to find out what this Wade guy did, then figure out where to go from there. There must be a record of what he was up to somewhere."

"Such as?" Suraj said.

"I have no idea."

But *I* did. Or at least I knew someone who might.

CHAPTER 33

On the plus side, Suraj had to work the next day and Dad was busy interviewing gay uncles for an upcoming bridal shower. It would be just the two of us.

On the minus side, Dalton couldn't get his limo driver at such short notice. We'd have to find our own way.

On the life-flashing-before-your-eyes side, Raylene had that all figured out. We'd take Albertina's car.

It was terrifying, although I have to admit, she was getting better. (Given that *terrifying* was an improvement, you can appreciate how badly she drove before.) She'd eased up a little on the brake and finally clued in to what rear-view mirrors were for.

"In my defence," she pointed out, "you rarely have to change lanes on a tractor."

I wanted to ask her about tractors and how she knew how to drive one and see what that would tell me about her life, but I'd promised I wouldn't. The night before, we'd collected a bunch more random files from

Albertina's apartment, then walked Suraj home. We talked him into storing them at his place for safekeeping—not easy to do given his fondness for conspiracy theories—then found ourselves alone again. I let her lead the way, and pretty soon we were in front of my apartment building.

"I'm new to this," I said, "but isn't the guy supposed to walk the girl home?"

"What century are you from?" she said.

"I'd like to walk you home. I'd like to know where home is for you."

"Yeah, well, too bad. A girl has to have her secrets."

"What century are *you* from?"

"Seriously," she said. "Would you quit bugging me about that?"

"Why?"

"Because if you don't, I'm leaving. Like, for good. If you do, I'll stay and maybe we can get to the bottom of this Schmidt thing together. Deal?"

What was I going to say? "Deal."

"Shake?" She held out her hand.

"No." It was like a giant leaf blower had cleared out my insides and I was totally hollow. "Kiss?"

"Deal," she said, although it didn't actually happen. I'd just figured out what to do with my arms when she went, "That car."

172

"What car?"

"That one." She pointed at a black sedan with tinted windows suddenly speeding up past us. "It's following us."

"Sure?"

"Yes. I saw it at the funeral. It's Schmidt's."

"Sure?"

"Would you quit saying that? Like I have to be one-hundred-percent positive about everything? Go with your gut. That's what Albertina would do. And my gut is telling me that was Schmidt, or at least one of his henchmonkeys. I think I should take a cab."

"I think you should too," I said, figuring we had that settled and we could get back to the business at hand, i.e., the kiss, but just then, out of nowhere, a stupid cab appeared and Raylene threw out her arm and it stopped and she hopped in, and the only kiss I got—if you could even call it that—was a little brush on the cheek before she slammed the door and zoomed away. I get more action from the old ladies at baptisms.

I wasn't going to blow my chances of collecting on that kiss by bringing up her family now.

Instead, I told her what I'd found out after she'd left that night and I'd googled Schmidt.

"Nothing."

"Nothing? Like, *nothing?!*"

I had to physically turn her head back towards the road.

173

"Well, not totally nothing. But not much more than we got from that file. He grew up here. Got an MBA from University of New Hampton. Married. Divorced. Started a bunch of businesses. Sold some. I checked out their websites too. They all looked, I don't know, normal, least to me. I couldn't find anything bad about him anywhere."

"Well, Albertina must have. Someone's got to know something."

"Which is exactly why I'm risking my life right now by letting you drive me to Dalton's."

Raylene laughed. We both did.

There aren't many times in life when you're simultaneously ecstatic and absolutely convinced you're going to die, but this was one of them. We were careening up the highway towards the prison. I was giving Raylene directions and watching for oncoming traffic and feeding her little bits of granola bar in the hopes that she'd keep both hands on the wheel.

She pulled up at the end of the prison gates. She fixed my tie and promised to drive safely—"or at least safely-ish"—then headed off to the Chow Hound Café in town. She'd wait there while I grilled Dalton, then come back for me in about an hour.

The guards were surprised to see me without Dad. I had to fabricate an excuse on the spot to explain, a) why he wasn't there, and b) why he couldn't know I was. I was proud of myself. Papa D and I were apparently planning a surprise forty-fourth birthday party for him. McInerney and Whitton didn't even seem to question the fact that Dalton wouldn't be able to join the festivities until Dad was well into his fifties.

I told Dalton the whole sad dead-Albertina-sleazy-Schmidt story. (The great thing about having a convict for a "grandfather" is that you can't shock him. I could have confessed I'd just held up a preschool fudge sale with a flame-thrower and he wouldn't have batted an eye.) He leaned back in his chair with his hands cradling his basketball-belly and listened quietly until I was done.

"You're in trouble," he said.

"You know Schmidt?"

"No, not personally, but I remember the case. Vaguely anyway. Late seventies maybe, early eighties. Some sort of investment scam. He'd talk some poor sucker into investing with him, then get that sucker to talk his friends into investing, who'd talk their friends into investing, et cetera, et cetera. Only problem was the company they thought they were buying into didn't actually exist. People lost their life's savings. They took Schmidt to court, but, as I recall, he got off on some type of loophole. Just a young whippersnapper at the time but a clever guy. I shouldn't say this—I gotta at least try to *look* remorseful if I ever want to get out of here—but I kind of admired him."

"So why am I in trouble then?"

"Well, in my experience, there are two types of people who get into this line of business. Greedy idiots such as myself, who end up in jail. And greedy psychopathic idiots such as Mr. Schmidt, who end up rich. He's not a nice man. Be careful. I wouldn't want to have to hire myself a new grandson."

"What about Albertina Legge? Did you know her?"

He polished his bald spot with his hand and thought about it. "Nope. Isn't ringing a bell. And that's a name I'd remember too. Look. I'll check out the law books in the library here and see what I can come up with. I'll even wave my standard prison wages of $6.90 a day, considering you're family and all."

"Email me when you find something?"

"Email you? What do you think this is, boy? The Google campus? High tech around here means an ever-sharp pencil. This'll be coming to you old school. Watch your mail box."

I thanked him.

"And your back. I repeat, Schmidt's not the type of guy you want to mess with."

CHAPTER 34

I told Raylene everything Dalton said. There was a little erratic driving until I managed to calm her down, but otherwise the ride back was relatively uneventful. Parking was a different matter. She mixed up the accelerator with the brake and rammed into a lamp pole at the far end of the supermarket parking lot. We lurched into reverse, then the engine coughed once and died.

"Oops," Raylene said when she realized the car wasn't going to start again. "Oh, well. Least you won't have to worry about me driving anymore."

Good thing. Only so much my nerves could take. I was freaked out enough with Dalton calling Schmidt a psycho.

"Hungry?" she said.

"Yeah, but I got to go. It's pulled-pork poutine day."

"A well-known national holiday."

"No, Dad and I always go for poutine on Mondays."

She leaned against the car door and looked at me funny. "Why do you always say it like that?"

"Whaddya mean?"

"'Dad.'"

"That's his name."

"No. You always say it like . . . '*Dad.*'" She made air quotes.

"It's that obvious?"

She did that *duh* thing with her face. I laughed.

"You know, weird, but I actually used to call him Will until I was about eight or something. Then my mother tried to get custody of me and we thought it would be a good idea if I called him Dad. Make him sound more legit. Impress the judge or something."

"We?"

"What?"

"*We* thought it would be a good idea to call him Dad? What's an eight-year-old doing making a decision like that?"

"Bingo! That's why he's Dad-In-Quotation-Marks. I love him and everything but. Well. If you knew him, you'd understand."

"I'd like to."

"What?"

"Get to know him."

"Right." I tossed a granola crumb at her. "I can't even ask where you're from, but you want to do the whole *meet-the-parents* thing with me? You got some nerve."

"Yeah . . ." She tossed it back. "You're right. That's not fair. Even by my standards."

I should have realized that had been too easy.

We arranged to meet the next day to figure out what was up with Janie and the daycare—we still hadn't a clue why Albertina had called her "the big one"—then we got out of the car. I waited until absolutely everybody in the parking lot, on the road, or in the supermarket was looking the other way, then I took Raylene's hand. She tilted her head and smiled at me. I figured that meant it was okay to kiss her.

Then my phone rang.

I tried to ignore it but 5:45? On a Monday? It would be Dad. If I turned the phone off, he'd go Code Red on me. If I didn't answer and let it ring, there's no way my lips would actually have puckered. Or maybe unpuckered. Whatever. (I figured for this to work, I needed them to do both.)

"Ah. Sorry." I shrugged. "It's DIQM."

It took her a second to figure it out. She laughed but didn't let go of my hand. "Go on. Take it."

Dad said he was running about ten minutes behind. He made me promise to get to the restaurant on time or we wouldn't get in. "I'm going," I said.

"Don't be late," he said. Monday is coupon night. It's busy. He gets nervous.

179

Raylene screamed, "Hi, Mr. Redden! Helloooo!" and I tried to shake her loose and walk away, but she really wasn't letting go of my hand now.

Dad went, "Who's that?" and I said, "Nobody," which got a big guffaw out of both of them. "Just some person I met at—"

Raylene grabbed the phone and bolted. Before I could grab it back, she'd managed to introduce herself and wrangle an invitation to dinner at our place for the next night. She shouted, "I'll bring dessert!"

"Soooo . . . now I know what you've been up to." Dad sounded authentically fatherly for, like, the first time ever.

"Yeah. Whatever." I hung up and tried my best to glare at Raylene.

"What?" she said. "It'll be fun."

"You can't be trusted," I said.

"You just figured that out?"

She laughed, so eventually I laughed too. She was holding my hand again and maybe even blushing a bit, and I seriously considered kissing her then, but there was an old couple right beside us now, putting groceries into their car at a speed of approximately one can of creamed corn per minute, and it would have been too embarrassing.

And anyway, Raylene still kind of scared me.

I gave her a little wave and I walked away.

CHAPTER 35

We figured we'd keep it simple. Pretend that nothing had changed, that we just wanted another look before we made our big decision about where to put Granny. I was worried Janie might get suspicious if two kids were in charge, so I got Kev to come as Albertina's son. He even did it for free. (He'd taken a bit of a shine to her after all the good things Reverend Muncaster had to say at the funeral.)

We got to Time of Our Lives Adult Daycare just before three. Janie opened the door, big smile on her face, and invited us in. The first few "guests" had already arrived and were working on their art projects. Janie helped an old guy with a runny eye choose a bead for his dream catcher, then asked us how our grandmother was. Kev said she'd "had a bit of a bad spell," which, I admit, was somewhat of an understatement, but the truth wouldn't have gotten us where we needed to go.

We started to explain why we were there. Janie stopped us, her eyes suddenly sad. She took us aside.

"I'm really sorry but I got some bad news the other day, and, well, I'm not going to be able to offer your grandmother a place—or anyone else for that matter. The church is being sold. I've been using this space for free, but the new owners have evicted me. I have to close down the daycare. I'm doing my best to find spots for everyone. I'll certainly keep your grandmother in mind but it might be tough. Not many places like this in the city."

She invited us to stay for tea and cookies, but I felt bad eating her stuff when she was going to be out of work soon and everything. We said thanks and left.

Kev had to run. He had a divorce hearing (his own) at four. He caught a cab. Raylene and I walked.

"So?" she said. "You think this problem just took care of itself, or should we keep digging and find out what Janie's really up to?"

I didn't think either. "There's a third possibility, you know. Albertina could've been wrong."

I felt sort of bad even suggesting it, her being dead and all. But she'd been wrong about Dad and me. Why couldn't she have been wrong this time?

"Janie just seems so, I don't know, good or something," I said. "The people there look happy. The place is nice. Didn't she say we wouldn't even have to pay if we couldn't afford it? I just don't see what her scam is."

"Yeah. Me neither. But people are cagey. That's how they get away with stuff. Acting better than they are. Still . . ."

"Still, what?"

"I don't know. Either Albertina made a mistake and we should drop it, or Janie's an even better liar than Schmidt. Frankly, I can only take one evil nutcase at a time."

I nodded. That was actually a little *more* than I could take.

We decided not to worry about Janie until we'd dealt with Schmidt, then Raylene said she had to go see about dessert. She leaned up, kissed my cheek, and walked away.

I stood watching her go and kicking myself for being such a spineless wuss, then I just thought *get over it*.

I went, "That doesn't count."

She turned around, smiling. "What?" She kept walking backwards. "Not good enough for you?"

"No, frankly, it wasn't."

She laughed. "Well, I'll see if I can do better next time."

Then she left and I just stood there with my tongue between my teeth and my hands in my pockets and my insides jumping around like a basket full of puppies.

CHAPTER 36

Raylene was off getting dessert. Dad was in his bedroom. I was pretending to watch TV while desperately trying to concoct some way to make sure this dinner didn't happen.

When I was little, I swallowed a Lego wagon wheel so Dad would miss a parent–teacher meeting. I considered doing it again.

"So? How's this?" Dad was standing in his doorway wearing a blue suit, white shirt, and paisley tie.

"You anchoring the news tonight or something?"

He looked down at his outfit. "I see what you mean." He went back inside.

I started digging behind the sofa cushions for something big enough to send me to the emergency room, but not big enough to kill me.

"This any better?" He was back. Khaki pants, polo shirt, and dock shoes.

I sighed. "Dad-In-Quotation-Marks."

"Ooh. Very Suraj-esque of you, but whatever does it mean?"

"It means you're pretending to be Dad. You're giving me the full fifty-bucks-an-hour-Almost-Family-Deluxe-Dad package."

"Only the finest for my boy!"

"Would you quit it? If we actually have to go through with this tonight, could you just be, like, Dad? For once?"

Quizzical expression. "Houston? Houston? I'm losing you."

"As in Will. Be yourself. You are off-duty tonight. Wear whatever best expresses the real you."

He put his fingers and thumbs together and bowed like this was all some big Buddhist joke, but I knew he got it. A few minutes later, he came back out in a *Pulp Fiction* T-shirt and baggy shorts he'd had since his weight-loss surgery.

"Ladies and Gentlemen—the one, the only—Will Redden!!!!!!" He shook his hands in the air and waggled his head around as if a crowd of Muppets were going crazy for him.

I closed my eyes and sighed. This was going to be a disaster.

Dad made fettuccini Alfredo (the only thing he

knows how to make). I emptied a bag of salad into a bowl and shook up a bottle of dressing. Then I sat on the futon and watched DVDs of *Up to No Good* while Dad did crunches on the floor. We were both nervous.

Raylene showed up half an hour late with a s'mores fudgecake big enough to feed a professional football team. She was wearing the dress she'd had on when she'd missed Albertina's funeral only she'd torn off the sleeves and the bow and made it shorter somehow too. It actually looked pretty good. It actually looked like something she'd wear.

We put the toaster and the unopened mail on the floor and ate at the kitchen table. Dad eventually relaxed enough to ask Raylene questions about her family. I thought maybe we'd finally hear about her brother, but she just said she was an only child and how much she was enjoying the fettuccini.

Dad spent some time rearranging the noodles on his plate, then he said, "So, how'd you two meet?"

I looked at Raylene and she looked at me, and I realized with horror that we should have synched our stories before she got there. That's Almost Family 101.

"I heard about him from someone and decided I had to meet him, so I looked him up." Vague and not quite a lie and kind of flattering too.

186

Then she asked Dad about what I was like when I was little, which normally would have been unbelievably painful but was actually kind of perfect.

He told her all sorts of exaggerated stories about my many exploits, including the Lego-swallowing episode, the time I smuggled a Popsicle out of a store in my diaper, and how I'd got my head caught between the railings on my first day of junior high and the principal *literally* had to butter my ears to get me out. (Actually, if we're going to be literal about it, it was margarine.) It was like his Greatest Hits album, but it worked. He and Raylene seemed to be enjoying themselves immensely. I got the feeling both of them were happiest when not having to stick to the absolute truth.

Dad called a cab for her when it was time to go and said goodbye. We sat outside on the front steps and waited. It was dark. No one was around. She was in a good mood. This would have been the perfect time for a kiss, but there was that black car again, idling outside our building. It hovered long enough to make sure we saw it, then it crawled away.

"Gulp," I said, like I was making a joke about what a chicken I was instead of just admitting it.

Raylene snorted. "Schmidt doesn't scare me. He's trying to intimidate us because he doesn't have anything better to do since his restaurant closed down." We had a good chuckle at that.

I croaked out, "He poisoned me!" in this feeble old-lady voice, which I realize sounds kind of insensitive, making a joke about it so soon and everything, but Raylene laughed. We both knew Albertina would have been crazy-cackling-over-the-moon-thrilled to see all those bright-yellow Health Department WARNING stickers plastered across Lorenzo's big, fancy windows.

"Gotta love her." Raylene bumped shoulders with me but didn't bump away. Her arm was bare and so was mine, at least from the elbow down, and our skin was touching. I felt like I had asthma or something. I was breathing but not getting any oxygen. Didn't matter. I'd just have to make do with the air I had. I turned towards her.

The stupid cab arrived. Raylene stood up.

"No kiss again tonight," I said.

"Nope." She started walking down the steps. "Doesn't look like it."

I shrugged like *big surprise*.

"Hey. I got an idea." She turned just as she got to the cab. "Let's see how long we can resist before doing it." She opened the door and got in. "Think how good it will be then."

"Two elderly people clamping wrinkled lips together. The thrill might kill us."

She laughed and blew me a kiss out the open window.

"Wow. Pathetic," I said. "You couldn't even resist for five seconds."

"That doesn't count." And she laughed again. Which was almost as good.

CHAPTER 37

It was a couple of days before the letter arrived from Dalton. (By special delivery, no less. As I said, the guy had style.) Raylene didn't have a cell so I just had to wait until she phoned to tell her. It was three whole days. We arranged to meet at the deli.

"Ooh, I love it! A real honest-to-goodness letter." She turned it over in her hands. "So quaint."

"Yeah. Until you read the return address." Suraj pointed at the words *Inmate #4270, Broadholm Correctional Institute.* "Kind of ruins the effect."

"Did you read it?" she asked me.

"No. Another thing I was seeing how long I could resist doing." I smiled. She smiled. Suraj said, "What?" then closed his eyes and went, "I don't want to know."

We scrunched into a booth at the back and read the letter together. Mostly, Dalton was just repeating what he'd said before. Schmidt had a company called Bulwark. There was an investment scam. A bunch of people got wiped out by it. They took Schmidt to court but lost on a technicality. Dalton wrote:

That's all I could get from the law books but I asked around. One of my "roommates" remembers Schmidt. He did some jobs for him ten years back or so: threatening phone calls, broken kneecaps, that sort of thing. Ernie hoped it might turn into a regular arrangement but then Schmidt decided to clean up his act. He wanted to give his mother something to be proud of. (He's apparently quite a mama's boy.)

There was some stuff about the various other businesses Schmidt got into—payday loans, a mattress franchise, and the restaurant chain we all knew about—but it wasn't until the very end of the letter that things got interesting.

P.S. By the way, I found that Albertina Legge you mentioned too. Believe it or not, I knew her. Quite a firecracker and a nice little figure to boot. The reason I didn't remember her is that she went by Tina back then and she hadn't married the Legge guy yet either. She and her first husband were the people who spearheaded the case against

Bulwark. He took the loss really hard. He'd talked his family into investing, so when he and Tina lost their money, the whole clan went belly-up too. As I recall, he killed himself shortly after the judgment came down. Tina took to drinking and lost custody of her kid. Sad story.

P.P.S. Dangerous felons such as myself aren't allowed on the Internet, but you may be able to find out more about her husband if you google him. His name was Elton (or maybe Eldon?) Aikens and he was quite a well-known country-and-western singer for a while.

I dropped the letter on the table. Raylene put her hand over her mouth.

"What?" Suraj said. "C'mon! What? The *Dawn-of-the-Dead*-zombie-face thing is kind of scaring me."

"Aikens," I repeated.

Raylene nodded. "Janie."

"Dr. Ewan? At the funeral? Asking about our big sister?"

Raylene slapped her forehead. "'Resort to the truth.' Remember Albertina saying that?"

"Exactly."

Suraj said, "I can't recall all the symptoms of stroke,

but I'm pretty sure garbled speech is one of them. Answer in a full sentence immediately or I'm slapping you both with the paddles."

"Janie Aikens really is Albertina's granddaughter," I said, more to Raylene than Suraj. He'd just have to catch up on his own.

"The big one," Raylene said, "as in *important* one, not bad one. That's why Albertina wanted to see her. That's why she needed us to find out everything about her."

And then I remembered something. I took out my phone and scrolled through the pictures I'd taken in Janie's office. Those old black-and-white photos on the back of the door? I found one of a big man in a cowboy hat, a small lady in a tight outfit, and a little boy.

"That's Eldon, Albertina, and their kid, I bet."

"Their kid. As in Janie's father," Raylene said.

"It's like trying to communicate with aliens or something. I'm getting out of here." Suraj left to clean off another table.

Raylene and I were both crying a bit by then and sort of laughing too, and I don't know if it was because we were happy or sad. I kept picturing Albertina with her wig off and her teeth out, holding Janie's hand, and looking up at her with tears streaming down her face.

"I thought she was acting," I said.

"Me too." Raylene leaned her face against my arm. "I'm so glad we brought her there. I'm so glad she met Janie."

Suraj walked past carrying a tray stacked with greasy plates and crushed plastic cups. His boss was watching so he had to look busy.

"Extra! Extra! Read all about it!" he whispered out of the side of his mouth and dropped a newspaper on our table. It was smeared with someone else's hot sauce and had obviously been read a few times.

The first thing I saw was a big banner ad and Schmidt's ugly face with the headline: "Lorenzo's: Open Again for Business!"

CHAPTER 38

The four o'clock rush at the deli started and Suraj had to get back to actual work. Raylene and I left.

We went and sat in a little park a few blocks away. We were too bummed out to go much farther.

She slumped against a tree and started yanking clumps of grass out by the handful. "This just pisses me off so much. It's bad enough Albertina died. It's bad enough Wade Piece-of-Schmidt gets away with ruining all those people's lives. But then they only close his restaurant for, like, five jeezly days or something? He's not even going to feel that!"

She was, like, clear-cutting the lawn now. "I seriously cannot *stomach* people who act all honest and smart and good, and underneath they're just some big, seething rat's nest of lies."

She almost hit me with the next clump. "Sorry. That's what I hate."

"Why?"

"Why?!" She leaned her head forward and let her jaw hang as if I was an idiot for even asking.

"I know why—I mean, of course that's bad—but really, why? You hate those people more than you hate, like, child molesters or rapists or something?"

"I don't know any child molesters or rapists."

"Oh. But you do know rat's-nest-of-lies kind of people?"

She turned away. I took that as a yes.

"Did someone cheat you out of bunch of money or something?" That would at least explain the tank top she wore almost every day and the cell phone she didn't have.

"No. Not money," she said as if I was incredibly shallow. "Money's not the only important thing, you know."

"Then what?"

She didn't reply. I ran the possible answers through my head. There weren't many. I mean, what else can you rip off a fifteen-year-old for?

"Love?" It was embarrassing but that was the only thing I could think of.

She did that little snuffly laugh of hers. "Yeah." She tossed some more grass. "I guess you could say that."

So much for any chance I had of getting that kiss. As if there'd ever been one. Who did I think I was? Like, look at her. Of course there was someone else. I started pulling out grass too.

After a while, she went, "I can't believe it." She got up and started running towards the street.

Towards the black car. It was idling near the sidewalk at the edge of the park.

The driver must have seen her coming. He tried to pull out but traffic was blocking the way. Raylene started banging on the window.

I ran down to stop her or maybe help her. I wasn't sure which.

She was going, "We know about you, Schmidt! We know what you did! Remember Al Capone? Remember what happened to him? We're going to get you!"

There was a break in the traffic. The car screeched off. She screamed, "You're so toast, Schmidt!" Then she turned away, put her head on my chest, and started to cry.

CHAPTER 39

It was only then that I remembered Albertina saying something to Schmidt about Al Capone. I didn't know what she'd meant and there was so much else on the video messing up my head that I'd totally forgotten about it. Raylene finally stopped crying and laughing and apologizing for getting snot all over my T-shirt long enough for me to ask if she knew who he was.

"That big gangster. A long time ago. The thirties or something. You know, with the hat and the machine gun in the violin case?" She took off her glasses to wipe her face and the sun caught the green stripe in her right eye. It was like a little tiny LED Christmas light.

"More random facts."

"Yeah, well, whatever." She was in no mood to joke. "I think Capone was the guy who did the Valentine's Day Massacre but I'm not sure. I just remember he was really violent. Everyone knew he was committing all these crimes, but they could never get him because all the witnesses were too scared to testify. Then the cops found out he was cheating on his taxes, so they stopped trying to convict him of murder or torture or whatever and went after him for that. That's what he finally went to prison for. Taxes."

It was starting to make sense. "So Albertina was saying to Schmidt, 'I couldn't get you on the investment scam but I've got something else on you. I'll get you for that'?"

Raylene put her glasses back on. "Sounds like it. Unfortunately, Schmidt's henchmonkey has the file, so we might never know. I just wanted to scare him into thinking we did. I figured that's what Albertina would have done."

"*The* file?" I said.

"What?"

"Like there's only one? If we're lucky, that's what he'll think too. But there were others in the black cabinet, you know."

"There were?"

Now her whole face lit up, not just that little green stripe.

We had to take the bus to Albertina's and it took forever but I didn't care. We got a seat at the back and I put my arm around her and she put her hand on my leg and we played makeshift Trivial Pursuit until we noticed the gas station and realized we'd missed our stop. We had to run about ten blocks until Raylene said her boots were giving her blisters, so I piggybacked her the rest of the way.

We snuck back into the apartment. The place was still a mess but somebody had left a vacuum cleaner there and a couple of boxes of garbage bags too. They'd be cleaning the place out soon by the looks of it.

We got to work.

There was one file in the black cabinet about Eldon's death and another about Albertina fighting for custody of her son, but most were about Eldon Jr.'s life after she'd lost him. She'd saved newspaper clippings about his high school band, his university scholarship, his wedding, the birth of Janie, her first-place prize in the Kiwanis Music Festival, her graduation, the opening of the Time of Our Lives Adult Daycare Centre. Pretty sad reading, but nothing to do with Schmidt.

It was getting dark. We closed the black cabinet. I figured it was time to just admit defeat.

Then the phone rang.

CHAPTER 40

Albertina had the ringer turned up to the Help! Fire! decibel range, but with all the junk everywhere, we still had to scramble to find the phone.

Just as we did, someone's voice came on.

Raylene went, "Where's *that* coming from?"

I put my finger to my lips. I'd explain later. Old people all had answering machines like that.

It was an old man's voice. "Tina?" He sounded like he didn't realize he was talking to a machine. "It's me. Don. Where the heck are you, girl? I've been calling all week. I found some pretty nice dirt on Schmidt. I think you'll be pleased. Gimme a call. You got my number. Well, nice talking to you!"

Raylene and I both stood there frozen for a couple of seconds, then I looked at her, she looked at me, and we nodded. I hit redial.

Don answered. I told him my name. He said, "Are you one of them telemarketer people?"

I said, "No. I'm a friend of Albertina's." Resort to the truth, I thought. "I've got some sad news."

You think old people are so fragile they'll collapse if you tell them something bad, but they're not like that. I guess by the time you hit eighty, you're kind of used to friends dying.

Don was a bit shaken up but he pulled himself together. "Sorry to hear that. I always liked Tina. Salt of the earth, that one, them getups of hers notwithstanding. Too bad she had to go so soon. Think she'd like to hear this."

"Could you tell us instead?" He hesitated, until I gave him the whole story. I told him we'd just broken into Albertina's apartment again and didn't have much time.

"Well, I won't keep you, then," he said. "There's a fellow goes by the name of PJ. Skittish as all get-out but he's the one with the info. He works at the Pet Warehouse. Said he'll be there tonight with the photos. Tell him Donnie Weagle sent you—but listen. He's scared. Doesn't want to be dragged into this, so you make darn sure no one knows what you're up to. Promise?"

We did.

"And then give Schmidt hell for me, would ya—and for all the other suckers he ruined too."

"That's our plan," I said, then signed off.

We'd only just made it to the elevator when the super came down the hall and headed into Albertina's apartment.

CHAPTER 41

Dad was gluing on a mangy beard when we got home. He barely looked up.

"Got a gig tonight?" I said.

"Retirement party. Joan Beaton's."

I nodded. I told Raylene to make herself comfortable while I checked the kitchen for something to eat, but she didn't move. She was looking at Dad, then blinking, then looking again.

"Will?" she said. "That's *you*?"

"It is indeed, my dear." I have to hand it to him, he totally nailed the British accent.

"I didn't even recognize you." She gave his grey hair a tug. "You are *mad* good at that."

"Have to be." He patted it back in place. "Can't have Joan's colleagues knowing she hired herself a boyfriend."

He strapped a little foam belly on under his shirt and corduroy jacket, then we helped him choose a tie stained enough to say "absent-minded professor" and he was gone.

I zapped some frozen burritos for Raylene and me. When I brought them into the living room, she was wearing a short brown wig, an old T-shirt, and a kid's hockey jacket.

"Do I look like a twelve-year-old boy?"

"You look like a fifteen-year-old girl pretending to be a twelve-year-old boy."

"Well, fix me then."

"Why?"

"So we won't be followed. That black car. You know. Could be out there right this second."

"I think you just want to play dress-up."

She laughed. "Yeah. And there's that too."

I found some grubby prepubescent boy clothes and sent her into my room to change. I'd finished my burrito by the time she came back.

"Better?"

"Can you see all right without the glasses?"

"Yeah."

"Take them off, then. And the nose ring too."

She did. "So?"

"Still not very convincing."

"How come?"

She was too pretty.

"Don't know."

I found her a baseball cap. She had her mouth full of burrito when I clamped it on her head, and some salsa spurted out and got all over her lips and down the front of her T-shirt. She went to wipe it off.

"No. Leave it," I said. "That's what you were missing. You're good to go."

"What about you?"

She tried to talk me into going as a girl, but no way. Raylene didn't need to know how easy I could pass. I went as a schleppy older brother instead because it only required a plaid shirt, some ratty shoulder-length hair, and a knit cap.

Turned out it was a good thing she made us go in disguise. She was right about the black car. Just as we left the apartment building, it drove by again. (It didn't even slow down. I was mad good at this imposter stuff too.)

Pet Warehouse was a big-box store at the end of the bus route. The lady at the counter told us PJ was working in "rodents" and sent us to the back.

A big guy with a thick neck and veiny arms smiled and said, "Help you find something?"

I said, "We're looking for PJ."

"That's me."

"Donnie Weagle sent us."

PJ kind of twitched but scrambled back pretty quick into employee mode. "How 'bout I show you the chinchillas?" he said, all cheery again. He led us to a cage in the corner.

"Aren't these guys the cutest little things you ever saw?" He took one out for each of us, then went, "I wasn't expecting kids," out the side of his mouth.

Raylene nuzzled her chinchilla. "Yeah. Something came up. Don says you got some dirt on—"

"Don't say his name." PJ's eyes darted around to see if anyone was listening, then whispered, "I got nothing to do with this. Understand? He can't know about me."

"He won't. Promise." The chinchilla was sniffing around as if my wig were a potential romantic partner. "So. What can you tell us?"

PJ made himself look busy by fiddling with the water thingy in the cage. "I used to work for him. Security. Did some stuff I'm not proud of, but the money was too good to quit. Then one day he asked me to be his muscle at a private dinner. Him and some of his fancy friends. It was in one of his restaurants after it was closed for the night." PJ's voice got louder all of a sudden. "Careful not to squeeze too tight, guys. They can bite."

He waved at another employee walking by with a cart full of chew toys. When she was out of earshot, he said, "Anyway . . . I get my break, pop into the kitchen for a bite, and what do I see? Birds. Pretty little yellow birds about the size of my thumb, necks broken, lying on the counter all ready to go into the oven. Couldn't believe my eyes so I ask the cook. 'Oh, yeah,' he says, 'songbirds.' He was cooking up ortolans! Almost extinct birds! And for what? Appetizers!" He took a big breath in through his nose and the veins in his neck pulsed. "But that's not all. Guess what else was on the menu?"

I'm a burger-and-pizza-type guy. I had no idea.

PJ had to struggle to keep his voice down.

"Shark-fin soup . . . deep-fried tiger testicles . . . and sea turtle, I don't know, stew or something. I just about threw up. Seriously. You know me . . ." We didn't. "I'm an animal lover. I didn't know what to do. The other security guy called me into the dining room to do a shift, and I had to stand there and watch those pigs stuff themselves on endangered animals. I quit a little while later."

"Don said you have pictures." I wanted to hurry this along, and not just because my chinchilla was currently peeing on me (which, if he was hoping to date my wig, was not helping matters).

"Yup. Got some with my phone when I figured everyone was too drunk to notice. Date-stamped March 15, 11:45 p.m., and tagged Lorenzo's Seattle. I wrote the names of the other guys on the back of the photos and what they ate too."

Raylene sounded almost gleeful. "Can we see them?"

A man and a preschooler raced by on their way to the snake cage. PJ smiled at them, then went, "These little guys have had enough by the looks of it." As he took our chinchillas from us, he left an envelope in my hand and whispered, "Put it in your pocket. Quick."

"Anyone else know about the pictures?" Raylene asked.

He shook his head. "Hope not. Printed them out at the Walmart. I never send things electronically. Don't want to leave a trail. I know what that man is capable of. Which is why I don't want you hanging around here any longer." He jerked his head towards the front door, all tough guy, and for a second I could sort of picture him working for Schmidt. "You better go. But check out the angora rabbits first. They just had babies."

We were too wound up to visit the bunnies. We had to force ourselves to wait until we got on the bus to look at the photos. Luckily, it was almost empty and we were right at the back, but we were still nervous. PJ was clearly terrified, and he was a big guy.

There were four pictures of a bunch of middle-aged men around a table. They had their jackets off and their sleeves rolled up and their plates piled high with food. In one of them, Schmidt had his glass up in the air like he was giving a toast.

I was really excited until Raylene pointed out the obvious. "The only thing this proves is that the guy knows how to eat."

"What do you mean?"

"Well, look." She pushed the photos towards me. "How do you know that's sea-turtle stew and not Rice-A-Roni or something?"

I flipped through all the pictures. She had a point. It's not as if we'd caught Schmidt biting the head off a live emu. This just looked like a particularly pathetic version of Boys' Night Out.

Raylene sighed and got up.

"I need to ask the bus driver something. In the meantime, have another look. Maybe I'm wrong. Maybe there's a clue here I'm missing."

I poured over every photo but I didn't see anything. I checked the back. We had the menu, the names of the guys—Len Pineiro, Mike Doherty, Dave Leibowitz—but no actual proof, especially since PJ didn't want to get involved. I shook my head and put the pictures back in the envelope. I looked up. That's when I realized Raylene had slipped off the bus without me noticing.

CHAPTER 42

Someone was ringing the doorbell.

I went, "Dad! Would you get it?"

No answer. I looked at my phone. 8:07 a.m. He'd still be at the gym. I put my pillow over my head and prayed that whoever was at the door would be attacked by wild dogs.

The doorbell kept ringing. If Suraj had lost the key to his apartment again, I was going to kill him. He couldn't just crash here whenever he wanted.

Unless, of course, he had food.

I realized he could very well have food, and I was hungry. I got up, stumbled down the hall, and opened the door.

And there was Raylene, smiling away.

I didn't smile back. I think I'd finally reached the point where I'd rather see Suraj with food than Raylene without.

"I wish you'd quit doing that," I said.

"I had to." She pushed past me. "You weren't answering."

"I don't mean ringing the doorbell and you know it. I mean ditching me."

"Sorry. Bad habit."

"Not funny."

"But true. And do you know what *I* wish?"

I sighed. This was going to be a joke.

"I wish you'd put some pants on."

She pointed at my boxers, then covered her mouth like she was shocked or something. I ran into my room to change.

I looked through the stuff on my floor for something to wear while Raylene screamed at me from the living room.

"I figured it out."

"What?"

"How we're going to get Schmidt."

"Oh, yeah?" My jeans weren't exactly clean but they were close enough. I pulled them on. "How?"

"We're going to do what Albertina would do."

I plunked down on my bed. I didn't like the sound of this.

"We're going to fake it."

It only took her a couple of hours to convince me. I tried to talk her into taking our so-called evidence to the police, but Raylene was right. What would they be able to do? Nothing. And Albertina deserved better than that.

We came up with our strategy, then stood outside the apartment building until the black car with the tinted windows showed up. We figured, sooner or later, it would.

"Our ride's here," Raylene said. She darted into the street and blocked its way before it could take off again. I ran out after her and opened the door.

"Take us to your leader." We said it together in a really bad alien voice. We'd planned that too. We thought it would be funny.

The guy apparently didn't think so, but he took us there anyway.

CHAPTER 43

"Terribly sorry about your grandmother." Wade Schmidt squeezed his carcass out from behind his massive desk and shook our hands. "I understand from the police she'd had a bad heart for some time."

"Cut the crap," Raylene said. Schmidt and I were both shocked. I don't know about him, but I'd been expecting more of an intro. "You couldn't be happier she's gone."

Schmidt managed to keep the pity smile on his face. "I have no idea what you're talking about. Why in heaven's name would I want her gone?"

"Bulwark Investments? That ring a bell?"

He pretended to think about it for a few seconds, then shook his head.

"Really? Hmm. Funny," Raylene said. "You owned it for eight years. That's how you made your fortune. Remember? Scamming innocent people out of their life savings?"

Schmidt would have made an excellent addition to our Almost Family roster. He barely blinked.

"You must have me confused with someone else. I'm a simple restaurateur."

"You're a simple liar, Mr. Schmidt."

"Schmidt?"

"Drop the Lorenzo business. We know all about you."

I was getting nervous. Clearly, no one had warned Raylene not to tease the psychopaths. Schmidt glared at her for a second, then settled back into his chair with a sneer.

"That was decades ago, and I was cleared of all wrongdoing."

"Not quite. Getting off on a loophole doesn't make you an innocent man."

"To you, maybe"—as in *snivelling little piece of nothing that you are*—"but in the eyes of the law, I'm a respectable businessman."

"Businessman. Yes. Respectable? I'm not so sure. But it doesn't matter. That's not why we're here."

"Oh, yeah? Then why are you?" He checked his watch. "But keep it short. I'm a busy man."

This was where I came in. "Do you happen to recall what you had for dinner March fifteenth?"

"March fifteenth?" He laughed. "I don't remember what I had for dinner last night."

"Well, let me refresh your memory. You and three of your friends were at your Seattle restaurant where you dined on roast ortolan, shark-fin soup, tiger testicles— which makes me kind of squeamish even thinking about, let alone actually chewing on—and sea turt—"

"This is a bunch of nonsense." Schmidt's forehead was dotted with sweat.

"Shall I escort them out, boss?" His security guy grabbed us. Schmidt clearly liked them big.

Raylene jerked her arm away. "Get your hands off me. We were going anyway. We're busy too. We've got incriminating photos to send to the media."

"And the police," I said, in case it wasn't clear.

Schmidt just stared at us for a couple seconds, then he chuckled. "You don't have photos. You're playing me."

Raylene shrugged as if she didn't care what he thought.

"I just realized something," I said to her. "He's got the same tie on he had that night." It was worth a try.

Raylene looked at him, then shook her head. "No. Sorry. I'm pretty sure he had a green tie on that night. There's that shot of him, munching on that itty-bitty tiny little drumstick? You know the one. I distinctly remember a green tie."

I conked myself on the forehead. "You're right. It was Len Pineiro in the blue tie . . . hold on. Is Len the bald guy? Or is that Dave Leibowitz? Anyway, it was the bald guy in blue . . ."

That wiped the smile off his face. The security guy got us each by the elbow again and had almost frog-marched us out the door when Schmidt went, "Stop. Stop. Bring 'em here."

He looked back and forth between the two of us, then he said, "All right. What's your angle?"

"How do you know there's an angle? Maybe we just want to see you squirm." Raylene was loving this.

"I've been in this business since before you were born. I know how this works."

"Well, then, why aren't you getting out your wallet?"

"Are you blackmailing me?"

"Why, yes, we are." Raylene turned to me and smiled sweetly. "Wouldn't Granny be proud?"

CHAPTER 44

The ceremony was pulled together pretty fast but there was still a reasonable turnout from the press. The restaurant was almost full. (The free wine and appetizers might have helped.)

Some PR lady introduced him, then Wade Schmidt sauntered up to the microphone, big game-show-host of a smile on his face. He welcomed everyone, especially Raylene and me for making this possible, then launched into his speech. He talked about his humble beginnings and how he owed so much of his success to the older people who'd given him money to get started in business.

"*Given* isn't quite the word I'd use," Raylene whispered but we let it pass.

"That's why I'm so delighted," he went on to say, "to be able to present this award today to someone who cares so deeply about the welfare of our older citizens. Ladies and Gentlemen: Ms. Janie Aikens!"

Janie hadn't even realized she was in the running

for the Albertina Legge Small Business Award but, she explained, it couldn't have come at a better time. The money was enough for her to buy a permanent spot for her adult daycare centre. She talked a little bit about how she'd grown up without elders in her life and how she regarded it as a privilege to be able to live with and learn from them now.

Her boyfriend, Neill, was in tears by the end. So were a couple of the cameramen. The media finished up the hors d'oeuvre tray, then got on their way, but Schmidt insisted that we stay for dinner afterwards. On the house, of course.

We decided that some day, we'd tell Janie who her grandmother was, but not yet. We wanted her to enjoy her big night. And I think she did. We all did. Janie was funny. Neill was cool. They both played in an indie band called Not Exactly as Pictured. I'd worn my best funeral suit. Raylene was in her bridesmaid dress. We held hands under the table where no one could see. Everything added up to me being cautiously optimistic about getting my kiss that night.

Even though we were stuffed after the prime rib, Raylene and I shared a piece of blueberry cheesecake. (We forced ourselves to. It was ten dollars a slice and neither of us could see having that type of cash to blow on dessert for a while.)

"You look like you're wearing purple lipstick," I said, which I actually kind of liked but she got all goofy about it. She excused herself to clean the blueberries off her lips, but I wouldn't let go of her hand.

She looked at me and laughed, then leaned down and whispered, "Don't be dumb. I'm coming back." She still hadn't let me see where she lived, but she'd promised she would that night. She maybe sort of kissed me then—I don't know, her lips touched my ear, anyway—and left but I kept watching her all the way to the washroom.

That's why I was looking when the two cops walked up to her. She turned to see who it was, big smile on her face, then her eyes went huge and her mouth opened and she suddenly stuck her arms out straight and rammed right into them. The cops didn't even budge, so she tried to scramble past them, but those steampunk shoes of hers couldn't have had much of a grip. She slipped and took a table down with her. She was trying to crawl away on all fours when the bigger cop caught her by the hem of her skirt, then got an arm around her waist and pulled her off the floor. After that, her legs were just spinning in the air like a cartoon character's.

By that time, I'd shaken Neill off me and I was up and running towards her, but the other cop had his hand out in a stop sign and was going, "Stand back, son," like he meant it. "This has nothing to do with you." Even though it clearly did. Raylene was screaming, "Cam! Cam! Help me! Cam!"

Then Janie and Neill were behind me, trying to talk sense into the cops (at least they were on my side now) and Raylene was still screaming and struggling and biting, but it wasn't stopping them. They muscled her out the door and I heard Janie say, "What's happening? Do *you* know what's going on?" I turned around and there was Schmidt, all calm and concerned. "There seems to have been a warrant out for her arrest," he said. "How unfortunate. She was such a nice girl."

He ushered us back to our seats and waved for more wine, then he smiled and whispered in my ear, "A word of advice, son. Never scam a scammer."

CHAPTER 45

Dalton arranged for his limo driver, Fred, to take me.

Suraj had volunteered to come, but he couldn't afford to miss another shift at the deli. Dad said he'd come too. In fact, for a while, he'd kind of insisted on coming, but he eventually clued in to the fact that this was something I had to do myself.

"And, anyway, how much trouble can she get you into when she's under house arrest?" That was a joke. I tried to laugh. He said sorry and let me go.

It was a two-and-a-half-hour drive. Dalton had made sure I had lots of food and the latest *Grand Theft Auto,* but I wasn't interested in either.

Her name, apparently, was Hannah.

Hannah Jean Sutherland. Jean, after her grandmother. Who she'd lived with. Until she'd taken off, that is. She was back there now.

Suraj was the one who'd found out. I went crazy after the cops took her. I called the police station but they wouldn't tell me anything, and there was nothing on the news, other than a couple lines about a teenaged girl being arrested for car theft and several counts of break-and-enter. She was a minor so they didn't give her name.

Some time later, Suraj's mother had her regular bimonthly hissy fit and made him clean his quarter of the bedroom. He came across the files we'd taken from Albertina's. There was a MISSING poster in the pile, with the staples still dangling from when she'd torn it off a telephone pole. The girl in the picture had long, dark hair, no glasses, and no nose ring. Suraj only looked at the poster because he thought she was pretty, not because he thought it was her.

He also wanted to know if there was a reward, so he read the fine print. He saw that bit about the brown eye with the green stripe. He called me.

I called Dad. Told him everything. He lost it, big-time. Getting into a stolen car with a girl who couldn't drive and playing chicken with a well-known psycho-path apparently fell into the stupid-things-I-warned-you-never-to-do category. (To be fair, I didn't remember him ever saying anything about psychopaths.)

He screamed. He cried. He grounded me until I was twenty-one. And then he ate a whole tray of lasagna and calmed down.

He came into my room without knocking. He sat next to me on my bed. He put his hands around my neck and pretended to strangle me.

"You and me," he said, "we only have each other. Believe it or not, I can't just go out and rent myself another son—so you are not allowed to torture me like this. Get it?"

"I get it."

He repeated himself several times.

"Yeah. I know," I said.

He flipped my duvet over me, then rolled me up like a big breakfast wrap and sat on me.

"Why are you doing this? Would you quit it? I told you. I get it." My voice was all muffled.

He didn't move.

"Why am I doing this? *Why?!* Because I don't know what else to do. It's awkward, I know, but this is how I express my love, and also, of course, how I punish you for the hell you just put me through."

He sat on me for way longer than was funny or reasonable. It kind of hurt. Neither of us spoke. He always used to say, "No one gives you an instruction manual on how to be a parent." That much was clear.

I finally said, "Seriously. Would you get off me?"

"I'd sit here forever if I had to. You know that, don't you?"

"Yeah, sure. You're a real Horton Hears a Who."

"And you're a lippy, hare-brained, inconsiderate, ungrateful kid who almost got himself killed several times. But I love you more than anything in the world." He got off me. "I got to go to work."

He messed up my hair and pushed my face into my pillow. I let him do it, then I said, "Dad, I need to find Raylene."

"I'll see what I can do," he said and he left.

That night, he called Ryan Sumner, the cop I'd nephewed for last summer. Ryan did a little digging around and called back with info the next day, even though it meant he could lose his job. (Sometimes Almost Family people turn out to be better than family.) Raylene was apparently a runaway from somewhere in Guysborough County.

That's where I was heading now. I'd never been this far out in the country before. I didn't know if Fred was taking the scenic route or if all roads in the boonies were like this. There were actual cows in actual fields, walking around like they owned the place. I knew she drove a tractor, but it had just seemed like the type of quirky hobby someone like her would pick up, not something she'd have to do to survive or whatever. I couldn't believe that she was a real farm girl. It sounded so primitive, like saying she was a milkmaid,

225

or a wench, or a druid high priestess (although *that*, frankly, I could sort of picture.)

Ryan had told Dad her last known address in the city was St. Cuthbert's Youth Shelter. When I'd heard that, everything sort of came together for me. I went to Reverend Muncaster's office.

I sat down across the desk from her and she pushed a tray of Nanaimo bars at me. "Eat. Sally Fenton's funeral. Enough for an army. Now, what can I do for you?"

I told her.

She looked at me funny for a sec, then she nodded. I think that's when she sort of figured it out too.

"I *thought* I saw Raylene out back after Albertina's funeral, but then I said to myself, *couldn't be*. They didn't know each other, and anyway, that dress! The kid I knew from the shelter would never wear something like that . . ."

She always starts her sermons with a little joke. Loosens people up.

"I didn't know much more about her until the police called. I'd thought she was Raylene Butler. Just another runaway with a sad home life. I shouldn't say *just*—but you know. Raylene didn't give much away. I certainly didn't realize she was one of the Gooderham twins until the cop gave me the lowdown."

I went, "Gooderham?"

"Long story."

"I'm not going anywhere."

"Okay. But have something to eat, then." She pushed the squares at me again. "You've gotten so thin."

I ate. She talked.

"It was a famous court case around here, must have been almost fifteen years ago now, I guess. There was a car crash. The father was driving. He survived, just barely, but the mother was killed. Utterly tragic. The only thing worse was what followed. The two sets of grandparents got into a knock-'em-down drag-'em-out custody battle over the babies. The mother's side blamed the father for the death. Wanted to keep both children. The father's side felt it was an accident and so were, of course, enraged. Everybody was heartbroken. Everybody needed someone to blame. The judge eventually decided to divide the twins. The boy went to the father's people and stayed a Gooderham. The girl went to the mother's and became a Sutherland."

"Why did the girl"—I couldn't call her Hannah—"run away? Did they beat her or something?"

"Don't know. She never told me. They rarely do. And I don't ask. My job is just to make kids feel safe and loved while they're here."

"Do you know what happened to the brother?"

"I do now. After the Bounce Back fundraiser, I realized

she'd lost someone to suicide, but I didn't know the details. When the cops told me who she was, I googled the case just to refresh my memory. An obit came up along with the other stories. Jacob. That was his name. He was only fifteen."

She shook her head.

"Terrible. That family faced so much suffering. First the crash and the mother's death. Then the court case. Then the father, who'd been left paraplegic by the accident, died about ten years ago. And now the son kills himself."

"Do you know why?"

She shrugged. "Can you ever?"

Fred's voice came over the speaker into the back of the limo. "Last gas station for a while, sport. Need to take a leak?"

"Nah."

"Sure? By the looks of things, could just be outhouses after this."

I said, "Okay."

We pulled in. He filled the tank. I peed, washed my face, bought some Mentos, then almost laughed at myself.

Like she was going to kiss me now? Would she even be happy to see me? I had no idea. I got back in the car.

It was almost two months since the thing at the restaurant. I'd phoned every Sutherland in Guysborough until I got the right one. I kept calling, but she wouldn't come to the phone. I was hurt at first, and worried too, but then I was just mad. It wasn't my fault her brother died. Raylene had lied to me from the beginning about stuff. She'd ditched me over and over again. And, fine, she probably hadn't gotten herself arrested on purpose, but still. The least she could do was talk to me about it. The least she could do was explain.

I got the feeling that wasn't going to happen. I gave up calling.

But then Suraj reminded me how she'd thought Dalton sending me an actual paper letter was charming or quaint or something, and I couldn't get that out of my head. I wrote her a letter.

Dear Raylene—
    I'm coming to visit you next Tuesday. I won't stay long.
    Yours truly,
    Cam

It was only four lines but it took me ages to write because I agonized over every word.

Dear—too formal? Maybe, but I wanted her to know I was serious.

229

Raylene—or Hannah? No, it had to be Raylene. I knew lots of Hannahs. She wasn't a Hannah.

I'm—Okay. I didn't actually agonize over the pronouns or prepositions but the rest was torture.

Should I say I'm coming or ask if I can come? I wasn't going to give her the chance to say no.

Should I tell her the date? She might take off if I did. Might not be there if I didn't. I flipped a coin and I told her. At least she couldn't say she didn't know when I'd be there.

I won't stay long. I added that later. I wanted to make it sound like it didn't matter that much to me. Like I had better things to do. This was just a courtesy call.

Yours truly. That was the part that really got me. What else could I say? *Sincerely?* After everything she put me through, it sounded sarcastic. *Love?* No way.

We'd just turned on to a dirt road. The potholes made my fillings rattle.

So *yours truly* it was. That was fair. That's what I'd always been, even if she hadn't. She got the good, bad, and ugly of yours truly all the way through. I never lied to her. I told her the truth. I stuck to my end of the deal.

I poured myself a glass of juice and tried to calm down. I was so mad at her.

Then, I don't know why, I remembered her at the restaurant, her lips purple from the blueberry cheesecake, whispering in my ear, smiling as she got up to go to the washroom.

Fred came over the speaker again. "This looks like the place, sport. Want me to go up the driveway or leave you here?"

That's when I realized I wasn't mad at Raylene. I'd never been mad at her. I was scared.

CHAPTER 46

Fred parked at the side of the road and I walked up the long dirt lane alone. I hadn't known what to wear to a farm. Dad suggested a bunch of stuff but, seriously, what was he thinking? (Suraj summed it up best: Old-MacDonald-goes-a-courtin'.)

I put on my regular jeans and a clean blue T-shirt with "Restless Sidewalk" written in dark green across the chest. I had no idea what that meant. It was probably a bad translation from Korean or something, but it didn't sound offensive.

Suraj had dropped by before his lunch shift to see me off. He'd taken one look and said, "Average-teenage-boy-puts-on-something-comfortable." I'd nodded. That was more or less what I was going for.

Then I thought, "No." Not this time.

All my life, I'd just faded into the background. That was my job. To be the chameleon. Raylene was the first person who'd ever really seen me for who I was (other than Suraj and Dad, of course, but they don't count).

I was finally going to stand out. I was going to say to the world, or at least Raylene, that this is me.

I put on a red shirt. It looked stupid.

I went through our entire wardrobe department, a.k.a. the hall closet. I tried on a leather jacket, a vintage bowling shirt, a souvenir football jersey, a sweater that looked like a smaller updated version of the one Nu Luv had given Bloat, a striped shirt, and a tie.

I took them all off and went back to the nondescript Restless Sidewalk T-shirt.

I just had to hope my inner beauty would be enough for her.

I was almost at the farmhouse when a lady wandered out from around the side. Her grandmother, I figured. The one who'd said over and over again, "I'm sorry but Hannah can't come to the phone. May I take a message?"

Yes. Would you mind telling her that I'm sorry I ever met her?

I never said that, but I'd thought it. I thought about how much I missed her too, and about funny things I wanted to tell her or news I'd like to pass along about Dad or Suraj or Janie's new daycare, but I never did.

It had been really hard, especially when all the stuff kept coming out about Schmidt. For a while there, it looked like our brilliant blackmail scheme had helped him more than hurt him. Giving all that money to the Albertina Legge Small Business Award just made him look like the best guy ever and he milked it for all it was worth. There were ads everywhere about that stupid award. Who even remembered his restaurant being covered in health department stickers anymore? I kept thinking Albertina would be so mad if she knew. I was worried she was going to come back and haunt me.

I was really bummed out about it, so next visit to the prison, I told Dalton the whole story. It was just to get it off my chest, really, but he went, "Hmmm," like he knew something and I went, "Yeah?"

Turns out there was a guy in the next cell doing time for exotic animal smuggling who owed Dalton a favour. (I didn't ask why. Some things are better not to know.) A little more digging and some help from Ryan in the cop shop and, well, I'll be! Schmidt apparently also has a taste for the rare Chinese giant salamander. We don't have anything on him yet, but Ryan's confident we will. (Note to eaters of endangered animals: never mess with a guy in canine patrol. Or anyone scared of Albertina's ghost, for that matter.)

I was dying to tell Raylene, but no way I'd leave that in a message. Instead I just said, "No, thank you," and her grandmother said, "All right, then" and we both said bye and hung up.

Her grandmother had short, grey hair and baggy jeans and a mauve sweatshirt with a cow on it. She put up her hand when she saw me walking up the driveway, but that was as close as she came to waving.

"Cam, I guess," she said when I said hello. She wiped her hand on her pant leg and held it out to shake. She wasn't very big.

"Mrs. Sutherland," I said and shook it.

"Call me Jean. She's this way."

She led me to the house. It was yellow with brown trim and more or less what you'd think a farmhouse would look like. A pointed roof, a covered porch, a shovel leaning by the front window.

"Go on in. I've got some chores to see to. There's cake I made on the table if she forgets to mention it." She opened the door and hollered, "Hannah! He's here."

I stood on the doorstep.

She flicked her hand at me like *get going,* then she kind of mumbled something. I think she said, "It'll be okay," but she'd turned and walked away before I could be sure.

The kitchen was clean and bright and neat, but sort of crowded, as if nothing ever got thrown away. Lot of old people get like that.

I studied the chicken-shaped salt and pepper shakers on the back of the stove because I didn't know what else to do, then I heard the floorboards creak and I looked up and there she was.

No glasses. An inch of dark roots in her silver hair. The same plaid shirt but a different tank top.

"Hi," she said.

"Hi."

"Reverse skunk."

"What?"

Pointing at her head. "My hair. The way it's growing in."

I wasn't sure if that was a joke, so I just nodded. She smiled and I realized she'd meant for me to laugh, but it was too late for that now.

"Sit down?"

"Sure." I pulled out a kitchen chair and sat. She sat.

"Pound cake?" She pushed the plate towards me. Everyone was trying to get me to eat these days. "Nan's specialty."

"No, I'm fine."

She nodded. I nodded. Then she said, "Really?"

"What?"

"You're fine?"

I looked at the yellow stars on the tablecloth. What was I supposed to say to that?

"I'm not," she said. "I'm a wreck. I'm sorry. I'm sorry I screwed everything up, Cam, and I really miss you. "

"Why didn't you tell me what was going on?"

She held up her hands and her lips kind of trembled, but she didn't say anything.

"No," I said. "Stop doing that. You tell me. I came all this way. You tell me. Fair's fair."

She broke off a piece of cake and tore it up into smaller and smaller crumbs until finally she said, "Okay. How much do you know?"

"Some."

I told her what Reverend Muncaster said about the car crash and the custody battle. She went, "Yeah, yeah," until I was through, then she said, "But here's the thing. I didn't know any of that. I grew up thinking my mother got pregnant by some guy she barely knew, then she had me, then she died, and that was that. I lived here all alone my whole life with just my Nan and Grandpa. They'd lost their only kid and there was no one else around. I went to school every morning, and every afternoon the bus would drop me off at the very last stop and I'd trudge up the hill and spend the rest of the day with the cows and the goats and my two sad old grandparents.

"And that was fine, really. I mean it. Even after Grandpa died, I still had Nan. She's not the most lively conversationalist but she's always been good to me. Loved me like crazy. So, I mean, it wasn't like I was abused or anything. It was just really lonely. My whole life, I had this feeling as if my best friend had just dumped me. As if I'd had someone in my life who'd made me happy but they'd left me and now I didn't know what to do with myself except be sad. I remember saying something like that to Nan when I was little and, of course, everyone figured I was talking about my mother. That's what I'd always figured too.

"Then, four months ago or something, Nan and I were in town getting groceries and this lady came up to us. She went, 'This must be Hannah,' so I smiled and did this how-do-you-do thing and I could see Nan start to look all anxious. I put the cornstarch in our cart and was about to get something else when I hear the lady go, 'Jean,' really serious. 'I'm so sorry about your grandson.'

"*Grandson.* It was like the word had this power. I was suddenly alert and all, I don't know, jangly. The lady must have known she'd said something she shouldn't've. She went pink and Nan started babbling and kind of brushed her off and grabbed our cart, and next thing you know, she'd motored us out of there.

"I asked Nan about it, but she just kept saying, 'Marg's crazy,' and tried to change the subject, but I knew she was lying. When the lady'd said 'grandson,' I felt this thing. I can't explain it very well, but it was as if I remembered a whole other part of me. It was like hearing a song you used to like but forgot you even knew.

"I couldn't let it drop. I just kept at Nan until she finally admitted it.

"I was shocked. Stunned. That's the only way to describe it. I'd had a twin named Jacob Ray Gooderham and he'd lived two towns over his whole life, and I never even knew he was alive until he was dead. He'd probably been just as lonely as me. We maybe could have helped each other. Talked. Been friends. Fought. I don't know. Worst thing was I kept thinking maybe he wouldn't have killed himself if we'd had each other.

"I was so mad I just sort of snapped. I waited until Nan went to bed, then I stole four hundred bucks from her cookie tin. I hitchhiked into town. Cut my hair, dyed it, bought myself a pair of fake glasses so no one would notice my wonky eye, and got as far away as I could go. I ended up at the St. Cuthbert's Youth Shelter. It was just going to be a stopover, but then I found your card in the church parking lot and it seemed kind of like a miracle. You know, like, maybe I *could* have a family after all.

"Then I met you and Albertina and that seemed like more miracles. This, you know, cute boy who made me laugh and some lady who was going to fight for what's right no matter what? I felt like this was the place I was supposed to be my whole life."

"So why didn't you tell me?" That still really bugged me.

She looked out the window, bit her lip, and shrugged.

"I didn't trust you. Sorry. I don't mean to insult you. I didn't trust anybody. I kept on planning to tell you, then chickening out. I knew if the police found me, they'd take me back here and I didn't ever want to come back here. I was still so mad. I wanted to get away."

She swallowed. "I hope you didn't get in trouble. I'm really, really sorry I dragged you into this."

She looked down at her hands and rubbed the crumbs off her fingers, one by one.

"I'm not," I said.

CHAPTER 47

There's no coverage at the farm, so we can't email.

She doesn't have a cell, so we can't text.

The farm's two and a half hours away, and, at least until her court hearing, Raylene's not going anywhere. Dalton gave me another limo drive there for my birthday, but the guy's only making six dollars and ninety cents a day in the prison workshop. I can't be hitting him up for drives all the time, and there's no bus service, so we can't visit.

We call sometimes, but the only phone they have is in the kitchen and it's actually nailed to the wall, so half the time her grandmother's around and we have to talk in code. (That's kind of fun but somewhat limiting.)

So we write.

Like, actual letters. In envelopes. With the return address in one corner and some old dead guy scowling at us from the stamp in the other.

I like it.

I like seeing my name on the envelope and knowing that she wrote it. That her hand touched the pen that touched the paper that I was touching.

I like the words she writes and the words she scratches out and wondering why she changed her mind about them.

I like hearing about the farm and Nan and the sheep getting fleece rot and the goat getting blackleg and her court-appointed youth officer actually flossing his teeth during their last meeting.

I like the little pieces of her plaid shirt that she puts in every letter because they smell just like her and because it's time she got rid of that shirt anyway.

I like how she signs every letter *sealed with a kiss* because it reminds me of standing out behind the barn with the goat watching and the chickens ignoring us and her body pressed up against me, and her hands around my neck, and her lips.

But what I like most of all about Raylene is that when I'm with her, I'm actually me.

ACKNOWLEDGEMENTS

Thanks to my fabulous agent, Fiona Kenshole, for her enthusiasm, her hard work, her keen insights, and her lovely plummy accent. She makes even the need for major rewrites sound good.

Thanks to HarperCollins's wonderfully astute editor Suzanne Sutherland, for finding the stories and characters I'd missed in *Short for Chameleon*. It's a much better book because of her.

Thanks to the brilliant illustrator Kyle Metcalf for the gorgeous, engaging, and slightly mysterious cover. It's by far my favourite ever.

Thanks to the talented and gracious Teresa Toten for taking the time out of her whirlwind world tour as a bestselling, award-winning writer to not only read my book but to provide the kind review. She's as good a friend as she is an author, and that's saying something.

And thanks, too, to whoever wrote that little article hidden away in some magazine at my doctor's office about Japan's real-life rent-a-relative agencies. I owe you one.